"We may be the same species, but we don't speak the same language."

"Oh, we don't?" he drawled, edging closer.

"No."

Homer smiled and stretched an arm across the back of the couch, an arm that coincidentally landed right across Katherine's shoulder. She huddled a little closer to the armrest, whereupon he placed a firm hand on her knee. When finally they were sitting about as close as two people could get, short of climbing on top of each other—which Homer would have dearly loved—he nuzzled her ear.

"You know," he said lazily, "It's a funny thing about species."

Katherine froze. His breath caressing her ear was agonizingly pleasurable. "What's that?" she asked.

"They usually come in pairs. So even if they don't speak the same language, they can always find a way to communicate...."

Dear Reader,

Summer may be over, but autumn has its own special pleasures—the bright fall foliage and crisp, starry nights. It's the perfect time to curl up with a Silhouette Romance novel.

This month, we continue our FABULOUS FATHERS series with Nick Elliot, the handsome hero of Carla Cassidy's *Pixie Dust*. Under the influence of a little girl's charms and a mother's beauty, even a sworn bachelor can become enchanted by family life.

Love and miracles are alive and well in Duncan, Oklahoma! This little town with a lot of heart is the setting for Arlene James's brand new trilogy, THIS SIDE OF HEAVEN. The series starts off this month with *The Perfect Wedding*—a heartwarming lesson in the healing power of love.

In Elizabeth Krueger's *Dark Prince,* Celia Morawski accepts Jared Dalton's marriage proposal while tangled in the web of her own lies. But is it possible her prince has secrets darker than her own?

Be sure not to miss the fiery words and sizzling passion as rivals fall in love in Marie Ferrarella's *Her Man Friday.* Look for love and laughter in Gayle Kaye's *His Delicate Condition.* And new author Liz Ireland has lots of surprises in store for her heroine—and her readers—in *Man Trap.*

In the months to come, look for more books from some of your favorite authors, including Diana Palmer, Elizabeth August, Suzanne Carey and many more.

Until then, happy reading!

Anne Canadeo
Senior Editor
Silhouette Books

# MAN TRAP
## Liz Ireland

*Silhouette*
**ROMANCE™**
Published by Silhouette Books New York
**America's Publisher of Contemporary Romance**

For my parents,
and my grandmother, Dorothy Mayer McMurray

SILHOUETTE BOOKS
300 East 42nd St., New York, N.Y. 10017

MAN TRAP

Copyright © 1993 by Elizabeth Bass

ISBN: 0-373-08963-5

First Silhouette Books printing September 1993

All the characters in this book have no existence outside the
imagination of the author and have no relation whatsoever to
anyone bearing the same name or names. They are not even
distantly inspired by any individual known or unknown to the
author, and all incidents are pure invention.

®: Trademark used under license and registered in the United States
Patent and Trademark Office and in other countries.

Printed in the U.S.A.

## LIZ IRELAND

worked at jobs that ranged from actress to book editor before deciding to concentrate on writing. A former resident of Brooklyn, New York, she now lives in her native state of Texas with her two cats, Henry and Agnes.

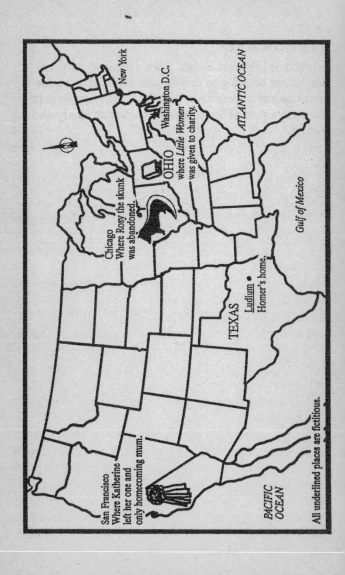

New York

Washington D.C.

*ATLANTIC OCEAN*

OHIO
where *Little Women*
was given to charity.

Chicago
Where Rosy the skunk
was abandoned.

*Gulf of Mexico*

TEXAS

Ludlum •
Homer's home.

San Francisco
Where Katherine
left her one and
only homecoming mum.

*PACIFIC
OCEAN*

All underlined places are fictitious.

# Prologue

"*Henry!*"

Bill Warren's familiar morning bark brought Katherine Henry bolting out of her chair and down the hall to her boss's door in nothing flat. It was nine o'clock on the dot, but as usual Katherine had been working like a Trojan since seven, swilling potent black coffee and achieving more in two hours than the average worker did in an entire day.

Which wasn't always easy, considering the fact that she barely slept a wink these days. After years of living in the nation's capital, the night sounds of Washington, D.C.—the *thudda, thudda, thudda* of rap music from cruising cars seven floors below, the wails of sirens, the screeching brakes of early-morning garbage collection trucks—seemed to have caught up with her. And now, added to her mental tally of sounds that could send her jerking upright at all hours, was an entirely new and disturbing one. A Great Dane puppy had just moved in upstairs.

Some good-samaritan organization had decided that elderly Mrs. Hobbs on the eighth floor needed a canine companion to make her feel happy and safe. And well she should, Katherine thought with a touch of bitterness, since the barking, clunky-pawed monster seemed to sense a burglar every ten minutes between the hours of eleven at night and six in the morning.

By far the worst upshot of her insomnia was the memory it sometimes brought of being stretched out in the back seat of her mother's old green Chevy, the tinny purr of the engine, the constant swish of slightly flat tires and the crunching of the gravel road beneath them lulling her to sleep. But accompanying those somnolent memories were ones of the loose, fly-by-night life-style her mother had inflicted on her while she was growing up.

No, she didn't want to think about those days at all. But still, sometimes she felt as though she would sell her soul for a good, three-hour nap in that Chevy...

"Think lively, Henry!" Warren snapped.

Katherine came to attention in front of Mr. Warren's large oak desk, but whatever he said next was lost as she took in the awkward contraption sitting before her. The structure appeared to be a plain pine box lined with chicken wire.

"What is it?" Katherine asked.

Warren looked at her impatiently. "It's an armadillo trap, but never mind that. It's the door that's the important thing."

Sensing her employer's urgency, Katherine focused on the small door of the trap. It had ordinary hinges attaching it to the frame on one end, and a compact metal box latching it at the other end, which Katherine pointed to. "You mean this, this . . ."

"Thingamajig," her boss finished for her. The man was practically dancing around the desk in anticipation of her reaction.

But Katherine still didn't see much to get excited about. "I don't get it," she admitted.

"It's a reversible latch!"

"Oh?" Katherine eyed the thingamajig a little more closely.

Warren eagerly demonstrated the gadget for her, using a pen tied to a length of dental floss. Slowly, with a practiced hand that allowed her to perceive every nuance, he put the pen inside the box, stringing the dental floss through the chicken wire. When he tugged, the pen was trapped.

"That's how a latch works, all right," Katherine said dryly.

"But wait!" Warren stuck his finger through the chicken wire and pressed a shiny tab. Then, ceremoniously, he handed the dental floss to Katherine.

"Pull on it," he commanded smugly.

She did, and to her amazement the latch made a small clicking noise and the door was released.

"Wow," she said.

It seemed as simple as a Slinky, as captivating as a child's windup toy. After Warren had given her another, hands-on demonstration, which revealed that the door could swing open and lock both ways, he let her take a stab at it. Soon, after hearing the magical click of the latch a few more times, Katherine was as enthusiastic about the little contraption as her boss.

"I tell you, this Homer Ludlum's a genius," Warren said. "No telling what new products can come from this."

"Homer Ludlum is the inventor?" Katherine asked.

"You're a lucky girl, Henry," he continued, eluding her question. "When the Boys asked me, I said you were just the man for the job."

By "the Boys," Katherine knew, Warren was referring to the executives of Patriot Games and Toys who inhabited the hallowed offices of the top floor. But she still didn't quite get the meaning of his comment.

"What kind of man were they looking for, exactly?"

"Not a man, Henry—a man trap." Katherine's stomach lurched when Warren opened his desk drawer and brought out two airline tickets. "We've offered Ludlum good money for his reversible latch, but he's not biting. Now we need an envoy."

"An envoy?" Katherine looked at the tickets with horror.

"Someone to go down and bring Ludlum bodily to Washington," Warren explained. "Not to deliver a sales pitch, mind you. We have three days of selling planned. All you have to do is get the man here for us."

"But I'm a deskman," Katherine protested with a twinge of pride.

"Not anymore. We're sending you to Texas."

"Texas!"

"Relax," Warren snapped. "It's just a day trip—a piece of cake."

Katherine gulped. "But why me? Surely—"

"This is a great opportunity, Henry," Warren replied, "See, we've looked into this Ludlum character. A real provincial, probably suspicious of strangers, like all those hicks down there. We want to present Homer

Ludlum with a view of a corporation with a friendly face. And yours is just the face we need."

"Isn't this rather odd, Mr. Warren?" Katherine asked. "I mean, couldn't we just hire someone to copy the latch?"

"Don't be cynical, Henry." Warren frowned dramatically. "The man has a patent, and the president, Mr. Wittington himself, wants this job done by the book. So we'll start on Ludlum tomorrow, wine and dine him this weekend, and by Tuesday we should be all wrapped up. If not, *then* we'll hire somebody to copy the latch."

"But..." Katherine nervously smoothed the jacket of her lightweight gray suit. Her job hung in the balance. She was flattered that the company had faith in her, but she knew deep down that their trust was misplaced in this instance. She would never survive a road trip. And impressing strangers was one thing she'd never had a knack for. Katherine said nothing, but Warren must have sensed her hesitation.

"Don't sell yourself short, Henry. You're my right-hand man, and this is your big chance to get yourself noticed. I've made reservations on a flight to Dallas for twelve-thirty this afternoon."

"Th-This afternoon!" Katherine sputtered. She couldn't believe she was arguing with her boss—she, Katherine Henry, the model white-collar soldier who never questioned orders. But she'd never been asked to go farther than the file cabinet and was perfectly happy being chained to her desk. Texas! This was exactly the kind of disruption she had tried to avoid her entire adult life.

Warren placed a fatherly hand on her shoulder and gave it a quick pat. "All you have to do is woo the guy to Washington. We'll take care of the rest."

"But what if he doesn't want to come?"

"Make him come. Flash your pearly whites at him, Henry. Bat your eyelashes. Tell him it's all expenses paid."

Katherine wasn't sure about the teeth and eyelashes part. She hoped her company wasn't sending her just because she was female! "And the wining and dining?"

"Don't worry about that. Just get the guy up here."

"But I've got to get somebody to feed my fish, and—"

"Put 'em on a diet," Warren said, steering her down the hall. "Oh, and Henry..."

Katherine turned.

"Better take a raincoat. Looks like they're in for some rain down there."

# Chapter One

**W**hy was a woman like that walking into Ludlum in the middle of a thunderstorm? Homer peered through the blinds of the *Ludlum Free Press,* watching the waterlogged stranger pick her way toward the Ludlum Gas and Grocery. His natural curiosity, which made him a successful reporter and part-time inventor, raced. Then he saw the woman's briefcase, and he realized what she was.

Another corporate messenger.

They weren't terribly difficult to spot. Over the past few months, he'd seen quite a few pull into the Ludlum Gas and Grocery, and they all had one thing in common—they looked completely lost.

This one, however, was on foot, drenched and appeared exceptionally frazzled as she hobbled toward the small store. From his view in the building across the street, Homer could see that the woman must have been dressed for success at some point during the day, but the heavy rain had done its damage. Her clothes were soaked through, her shoes were caked in the East Texas mud, and her hair was unraveling from the bun at the back of her head.

But something about the set of the woman's shoulders beneath her soggy, armorlike raincoat indicated she wasn't licked yet, not by a long shot. Homer felt the corners of his mouth tug upward. The folks those big businesses chose to send hiking all the way to Ludlum, Texas, to get dibs on his invention never ceased to amaze him. Always hopeful, confident that a small-town hick would sign on the dotted line when he saw a man in a suit waving a check in front of him.

Only this one was a woman, drenched and about to be disappointed, and Homer felt a little responsible for her being here. She wasn't half bad-looking, either, he thought as he glimpsed a flash of shapely leg before the woman disappeared behind the store's large screen door. Definitely worth a second glance.

He unfolded himself from his office chair and reached for his jacket. It was only gentlemanly to try to help the woman out of whatever mess she'd gotten herself into. Probably her car had broken down outside of town or maybe was stuck in the mud.

"You callin' it quits for the night, Homer?" Ephram Cake called from the next room. The old man appeared at the doorway moments later, stretching from the effects of one of his many catnaps. It was late, past normal office hours, but Ephram always said he preferred working late—sleeping late, was more like it, Homer thought—than going home and watching television.

"Nah," Homer replied. "I'm just going across the way for a minute, Ephram. Another one of those people have come for my latch. You just go back to . . . well, whatever you were doing."

"Okay, Homer." The old man walked Homer to the door. "But before you send that city fella packing, you might want to do an interview. Our Saturday edition's mighty thin."

Homer smiled. "It's not a fella, it's a lady. Looks like her car broke down, too. I don't think she'll want to stick around any longer than necessary, judging from the shape she's in."

"A lady?" Ephram's lined brow crinkled up in speculation.

It was true women were scarce in Ludlum. Especially ones who weren't on the elderly side or else already related to the men in town. Practically the only available female in a twenty-mile radius was Mary Lynn Baskin, the third-grade teacher, and heaven knew she wasn't much to look at. She'd probably be out of a job soon, too, since the town's population wasn't exactly on the upswing.

"Maybe you oughtta give this one a chance, Homer," the old man continued, peeking out the window. "The *Free Press* could sure use an injection of cash right about now."

Homer was still thinking about Mary Lynn Baskin, and not enjoying it one bit. Like every other swain in town, he had paid court to the town's lone bachelorette. It hadn't ended well, and it shouldn't have begun at all. Mary Lynn Baskin had no sense of adventure.

"We're doing fine," Homer finally answered.

"Well—" Ephram tugged skeptically at his suspenders "—we never did get that sign to put out front, you know. And just last week you said you could use another typewriter. And you could always do with more money for your research.''

That was no lie. Homer had been hoping to make it down to the Gulf of Mexico to try out his most recent idea—a weighted, oil-absorbent drop cloth that might be useful for oil spills. And he would surely be able to find some interesting folks down there to interview for the paper. Lord knew he'd been away a lot recently, but Ephram could take care of the paper while he was away....

Homer frowned. He didn't like to think about money problems. To his mind, just enough money was enough. Of course, he didn't know for sure that the woman had come for him, anyway. And she was pretty, now that he thought about it. His frown deepened.

''You just can't tell her to turn around and go back to where she came from, son,'' the old man continued. ''Not at this time of night. And not in this rain.''

Homer checked his watch. It was seven-thirty.

''I think I'll just go see what she wants, Ephram. I'll probably be right back.''

Katherine was getting nowhere with the two old men in the store, who were more intent on finding out about her than shedding any light on Homer Ludlum's whereabouts.

''You say you're from Washington?'' one asked. He regarded her from behind an antiquated cash register.

''Yes,'' Katherine replied.

''You work for the government?''

Katherine turned to the other man, who was seated on a metal folding chair by the door. But before she could reply, the register man barked at his friend.

"No, Abe," he said. "She said she works for some kind of toy company."

"That's right," Katherine said hopefully, feeling they were finally beginning to understand her mission. "Patriot Games and Toys. I'm looking for—"

"The one from the government was bald," the man said to Abe. Even though they ignored what she was saying, the two men never took their eyes off her, regarding her as two scientists would a specimen on a glass slide.

"That's right," Abe said. "That was last week."

"Last week?" The man's words caught Katherine's attention. "Do you mean Mr. Ludlum has had other business people visiting him?"

Both men chuckled. "Lady," the register man said, "there's been a steady stream of humanity coming through Ludlum ever since that armadillo catcher of his hit the market. You wouldn't think the thing'd cause such a fuss, but it sure has."

"Yup," Abe agreed, "it sure has."

Katherine's hopes plummeted. If the government had already gotten to Homer Ludlum, then she didn't stand a chance. She didn't even have a contingency plan prepared for this possibility. Mr. Warren had told her she had to get Homer Ludlum to Washington—period. But how willing would the man be to make the trip if he already had more money than all of Ludlum's other citizens put together?

She could hardly bear to contemplate failure. Exhausted from not sleeping properly for weeks, cramped from her trip and dispirited from slogging through the rain to get to a town that wasn't on any map she could find, Katherine was about as low as a person could get. Either she'd make Homer Ludlum return with her to

Washington or she'd hurl herself into one of those Texas mud puddles the size of Lake Erie and drown herself.

Abe's next words tempted her to do just that. "'Course, most folks who come down this way never even get to see Homer Ludlum."

"What?" Katherine felt on the verge of tears. Was she just another in a long string of lost souls who had come all this way only to discover that Homer Ludlum was some kind of crazy, unapproachable hermit?

"Nope," Abe's crony agreed. "Homer's not hardly in town enough these days to attend church regular, much less meet all the fancy people who've been comin' out here all the time."

"Where does he go?" Katherine asked, trying to keep the utter despair she felt out of her voice.

"I dunno." Abe scratched his head. "Where do you reckon Homer's always off to, Joel?"

"Beats me."

Katherine thought she would scream in the silence that followed, as both men appeared to ponder why anyone would ever want to leave Ludlum. She couldn't wait to herself. But before she returned to Washington she had to at least figure out whether Homer Ludlum was even in town. She asked the man behind the register.

"Sure he's in town," Joel answered, as if she was crazy to ask such a question. As if he hadn't just said that Homer Ludlum was rarely seen in Ludlum anymore. Katherine was beginning to think these guys were paid to scare hapless strangers away.

She took a deep breath and tried again, feeling as if she had come full circle. "Do you men know where I could find him?"

"Sure," Abe said. "We can tell her that, can't we, Joel?"

"No need," Joel replied. "He's comin' this way right now."

"What? Now?" Katherine tried to gather her wits. This was much too soon. She was a mess, and now that she thought about it, she wasn't at all sure what she was going to say to the man. But when she turned toward the door, even thought of speech failed her.

He was tall, much taller than she'd expected, and his lean frame filled up the doorway. His dark hair was cropped short, emphasizing the strong planes of his face. Dressed casually in jeans and a blue work shirt, he looked every inch a Texan, not at all the pasty, self-effacing, reclusive inventor she'd anticipated.

Immediately Katherine's gaze was drawn to his steely blue eyes. They were intense, but there was something warm in them, as well. It took a few moments for her to register that warmth as humor. He was taking in her appearance, too, and Katherine suddenly realized how horrible she must look in her wet, mud-splattered clothes.

"This here woman's come for your doohickey, Homer," Joel said.

Homer smiled inwardly as a blush crept up the woman's face. Even mussed as she was, she looked totally out of place in the shabby general store among the dusty shelves of canned goods and livestock feed. And he could just imagine the interrogation Joel and Abe had been putting her through for the past few minutes.

He extended his hand to her, and her eyes widened in surprise. It was a moment before she understood his intent and clasped the hand firmly in return, stammering out her introduction.

"I—I'm Katherine Henry, and I . . . well, I represent Patriot Games and Toys in Washington, D.C."

Katherine could have kicked herself. The statement had come out of her mouth sounding like a question, as if she didn't really know who she was. She wished she could have met Homer Ludlum alone, away from the prying eyes of Abe and Joel. But then, looking at the inventor once again, she decided she was rather glad the two old men were there. She pulled back her hand and smiled politely.

"How do you do?" Homer replied.

The room was silent. Homer could tell that this Katherine Henry was uncomfortable with their spur-of-the-moment meeting. She was even prettier close up, he noticed, even though she was a bit disheveled. And something about her was different from all the other representatives who'd come to Ludlum, other than the fact that she was female. He wished he could put his finger on it.

"So are you going to send this one packing, Homer?" Abe asked.

Homer snapped to attention. "Now, Abe, I've got to hear what the lady has to say first."

"Oh!" the woman interjected nervously. "I have a lot to tell you, Mr. Ludlum. In fact, I've come to make you a very attractive offer."

Homer's brow raised quizzically, and the two men chuckled. "I mean, Patriot Games and Toys is prepared to make you a very attractive offer," she corrected.

"Miss Henry," Homer began, "I really don't think—"

"Oh, but you don't have to think about anything, Mr. Ludlum. Patriot Games and Toys doesn't want you to make any kind of decision right away, knowing as we do how much interest your patented reversible latch has generated.''

Her statement puzzled him. "Then you don't want the latch?''

"Oh, no,'' Katherine countered. "I mean, of course. But the reason I'm here is to bring you to Washington, D.C., so you can see the company and hear our plans before you make a decision.''

There, Katherine thought, patting herself on the back. She'd given him all the necessary information in a pleasant, courteous manner in a matter of minutes. At this rate, they'd be able to catch the last plane out of Dallas tonight.

Homer barely heard a word she said. She talked so fast, so breathlessly, it was hard to keep up. Especially when the color of her cheeks had heightened so beguilingly with her rush of words. Close up, Katherine Henry seemed just a wisp of a person, dwarfed by her awkward-looking, masculine-cut woman's suit and an overcoat with Joan Crawford shoulder pads. But those clothes appeared to be the only thing holding her up through this ordeal.

She was much better looking than Mary Lynn Baskin, much more intriguing than any other woman Homer had ever met. And she was from somewhere far away; if there was anything Homer liked, it was traveling, meeting new people, talking to them and thinking about what they said and how they lived. He wondered how Katherine Henry lived, and realized she was offering him the opportunity to find out. He forgot about her corporate affiliation for the moment and zeroed in on something she had said.

Washington, D.C. He had never been there.

"I'll go," he blurted. He didn't know how long the woman had been talking or if she'd finished minutes ago and had been waiting in awkward silence for his reply. But judging from Abe and Joel's reaction, their raised eyebrows and shared glances, and from Miss Henry's own startled expression, Homer knew his impulsive words had surprised everyone.

Katherine wasn't sure she'd heard him right. He'd seemed to be listening to her, but for some reason she hadn't thought he really was. She suddenly remembered the crowning touch of her sales pitch, which she had practiced on the plane. "All expenses paid, of course," she added for good measure.

"Even better," Homer said. He had to get out of the musty air in that store. "Should we find out what's wrong with your car?"

Katherine felt her legs go rubbery. She had accomplished what she came to do. She would still be in Bill Warren's good graces and maybe she could convince him never to send her on a mission like this again. But now she had to confess.

"You did drive, didn't you?" Homer asked. The messenger was beginning to look a little sickly.

"Uh . . . oh, yes . . ." Katherine faltered.

"I saw you walking in and figured you must have had some trouble with your car. We can head out right now and figure out what's wrong with it."

"Oh, I know what's wrong with it," Katherine said. Taking a breath, she clarified, "I ran out of gas."

Joel and Abe collectively chuckled again, and Katherine glared at the floor, trying to control her rising ire. Obviously they thought she was a typical citified woman driver. Which was true in part, she admitted. She'd much rather go places on a subway than in a car, but she wished she could tell them that she had probably logged more miles in her short lifetime than all three of them put together. And that if it was up to her, she would never go anywhere, especially to God-knows-where in Texas searching for an eccentric inventor who had the bad taste to look like Gary Cooper.

When she glanced up, Homer was gone. Her eyes scanned the small store, but the man was nowhere to be seen. How could such a big person move so quickly? she wondered.

"Homer's out by the pumps," Joel said in answer to Katherine's questioning glance. He nodded his head toward the door. Through the screen, Katherine saw Homer Ludlum by one of the ancient-looking pumps she had noticed on her way in, filling a beat-up red gas can.

She stepped out the door just as he was screwing the lid on the can's spout.

"That way?" he asked, pointing to the road heading out of town.

Katherine nodded, and they began to trudge together through the drizzle toward her brown Chevy, barely visible in the distance. Somehow when she was at the car-rental place, a Chevy seemed to be the natural choice for her. At least it was something familiar.

"You run out of gas often?" Homer asked.

"Only when I drive." She had to half skip every few steps to keep up with Homer's long easy strides, even though she suspected he was slowing his pace to accommodate her.

Homer laughed. Her dry humor suited her, he thought, but he could tell she didn't find her situation particularly funny.

"I'm glad you decided to come," Katherine said. "When we get to Washington tonight—"

"We'll never make it to Washington tonight."

Katherine's heartbeat faltered. "Well, if we hurry, we could make it to the airport in two hours—"

"We'll never make it to Dallas in two hours," Homer countered. "Takes a good three hours," he elaborated.

Katherine sighed. It had taken her four and a half hours to get to Ludlum. He was right; they'd never make it to the airport in time for the last flight out. "I suppose we could stay at a hotel near the airport," she offered, shuddering at the thought. She hadn't stayed in a hotel in years and had hoped never to spend the night in one again.

"You can stay with my parents overnight," Homer offered.

"Your parents?" The idea sounded strange and a little too personal for Katherine's taste. "I wouldn't want to impose. Where do you live?"

"I live in the rooms behind the *Free Press* offices, across from the store."

"Oh," Katherine said, "that's much more convenient. Couldn't I just stay there?"

"Maybe if we were in Washington, but not in Ludlum." Homer considered himself a worldly man by Ludlum standards, but he knew that his small town would look askance at his keeping a woman in the newspaper building.

"Why not? I wouldn't be any trouble, and..." Katherine's voice trailed off. They had reached the Chevy, and Homer's steely gaze caught hers over the car's brown roof. Come to think of it, she wasn't sure she liked the idea of staying alone overnight with this man.

"Maybe your parents' house would be just the ticket," she said, then climbed into the car.

* * *

The elder Ludlums treated her as if she were visiting royalty. Ellie Ludlum, Homer's mother, insisted Katherine take her daughter Lacy's old room, which was the largest spare bedroom in the house. The room had all the mixed-gender earmarks of a tomboy. Katherine had had to shove aside a stuffed toy dalmatian as she crawled into the solid-oak bed and slipped under the pink eyelet coverlet.

From her cozy nest beneath the covers, she surveyed the room. Besides the fake furry animals that littered every available space, the only other true sign of the girl who had lived there was the lone poster of a rock star plastered on the back of the door. Katherine didn't even recognize him. She'd never been all that interested in contemporary music.

She'd never lived in a room long enough as a child to make it hers, either. After staying only one night in this room, she knew she would always regret not having a place that would hold her childhood memories, its keeper a doting mom like Ellie Ludlum. Her own childhood and adolescence had been spent in a string of boarding houses and cheap hotel rooms.

Her mother preferred a vagabond life-style, and she had littered the country with Katherine's childhood belongings. Her only stuffed animal, Rosy the skunk, had been accidentally left behind in the hotel when they left Chicago. A dried-up homecoming mum—the only one she'd ever received, since she was still the new kid in town when the homecoming games were played in the fall—her mother had convinced her to throw away in San Francisco. And her most prized possession of all, the copy of *Little Women* her father had sent her from Indonesia just days before he was killed on a training mission, was given to a Goodwill in Ohio. Katherine had protested bitterly over that loss.

"It was in French!" Marge Henry had retorted.

"Well, maybe Daddy wanted me to learn French."

At eleven, Katherine didn't understand any better than her mother did why her father had sent her a book in French when she was six, an age when the book would have been too difficult even in English. But she had always enjoyed looking at the pictures, especially the cover illustration depicting Marmie reading to the four girls in the candlelight, all of them looking slightly Oriental. And for five years she had dutifully packed the book with her things whenever she and her mother had moved.

"Your father didn't know what he wanted, except for me to stay put while he roamed the world," Marge had countered as she'd driven their station wagon down a Pennsylvania interstate, picking at the Passion Red polish on her nails. "Lucky for you, things have changed, Kathy girl. Maybe when you're grown up, you can join the air force, get sent to Indonesia and find yourself another copy."

Katherine couldn't wait to grow up, but the last thing she planned to do was join the air force. She wanted to put down roots, deep ones, and never again be in the position of watching her past disappear on the road unfurling behind her.

When she was eighteen, she said goodbye to her mother in Washington, D.C., and finally put down those roots, working her way through college and landing a job with Patriot Games and Toys, where she had worked for four years. She had seen her mother very infrequently, especially after Marge had married a trucker and henceforth never stayed put.

A tentative knock at the door brought Katherine out of her brooding. "Come in," she answered, not knowing who to expect.

The door opened and closed quickly, and before she knew what was happening, Homer Ludlum's tall frame was towering over her bed, a glass of milk in his hand. A glass of milk?

"Mother asked me to bring this up to you. She and Dad went to bed while you were still in the bathtub."

His tone implied that he had been speculating about what exactly she'd been doing in the tub for such a long time. Katherine felt the color drain from her face, remembering that she had actually nodded off during her bath. She decided not to give him any explanation.

"You Ludlums sure know how to treat people," she offered instead. "Bubble baths and warm milk."

"The bubbles were my idea," Homer said thoughtfully, easing himself down on the rocker not far from the bed. He tried not to notice how the nightgown Katherine had borrowed from his mother draped off her shoulder in an innocent but provocative way.

Katherine scowled as she digested his statement. Something about having this very virile Texan picking out her bubble bath disturbed her. And he was sitting rather too close now, his lankiness spilling out of the rocking chair and his blue eyes bright and intense in the subtle light of the bedside lamp. She was beginning to feel like Bill Warren's sacrificial lamb; she hoped Homer didn't have any funny ideas about her reasons for being here.

She tugged the eyelet coverlet a little higher, up to the top of her shoulders. When she saw that he had noted her protective gesture, she blushed. *He's just bringing a glass of milk, like his mother told him to.*

"That was nice of you. The bubbles...and the milk," she mumbled, trying to keep the wariness out of her voice.

*She was afraid of him.* Sensing her nervousness, Homer rocketed out of his chair and moved a safe distance away from the bed, then leaned casually against the dresser.

"Well," he began, to assuage her worries, "all we had for bubbles was dishwashing liquid, and that's what you got I just figured a thing like you would need bubbles or something. And that milk—" he nodded to the glass on the bedside table "—I should warn you, is goat's milk. Personally, I can't stand the stuff."

Katherine flinched at his change in tone, then watched as he made his way to the door in two easy strides.

"I have to be getting home now," he said. "Good night, Miss Henry." Homer nodded politely, then slipped out of the room as fast as he had come in.

Feeling inexplicably slighted but relieved to be alone again, Katherine relaxed her white-knuckled grip on the covers and sank against the pillows.

He was only being friendly.

*A thing like you.* Those were his words to describe her. While she feared he had designs on her body, he had been thinking of her only as a thing, like his reversible latch. A object to puzzle out. That realization made her feel more secure somehow. He was just glad to have thought of that bubble bath, she decided, much as he would have been glad to remember to change the oil in his car.

She reached for the glass of milk and noticed a picture of the Ludlum family on the nightstand. The daughter, Lacy, must have taken it, because she was nowhere in evidence in the picture. Ellie and Homer's father, Al, stood like bookends on either end of four boys. But Homer, the tallest, stood slightly apart from the rest, looking off to the side, staring at something beyond what the frame could contain.

She turned out the lights and nestled under the covers, wondering what Homer had been looking at. Before she knew what was happening, she was asleep, soundly, for the first time in weeks.

## Chapter Two

The next morning Homer stalked the area outside his parents' home, wondering what was going on inside. When he called his mother from his place earlier, she had said that Miss Henry was still asleep. How could she sleep past nine when she had a plane to catch?

When Ephram had come in that morning, Homer had told him to mind the paper while he was gone. The Saturday edition was going to be thin, and there probably wouldn't be another edition until Homer got back. He felt bad about that, but the *Ludlum Free Press* had always been a periodical in the truest sense of the word.

Ephram was used to taking over the paper during Homer's absences. Since there was rarely anything too newsworthy going on in Ludlum, Homer usually had to travel to surrounding areas to find material. Meanwhile, Ephram would crank out the obits and, more rarely, the birth and wedding notices.

The old man had been especially understanding this time, explaining that he'd gotten a glimpse of the Washington woman the day before. He'd also received a firsthand account from Joel and Abe of what had taken place in the store. Joel had pronounced Katherine Henry to be not half-bad for a Yankee lady, and Abe had agreed, adding that the woman was muddy, but overall a good-looker.

Homer was quick to explain to Ephram that his going to Washington had nothing whatsoever to do with Miss Henry's physical appearance. To himself he also noted that it had nothing to do with having seen her in bed.

He should have left that milk in the refrigerator. All the way up to her room, he'd halfway hoped she'd be asleep. But he liked talking to people, and since she was up past the time when everyone else had gone to bed, he'd hoped she was a night owl, like him.

But all he'd done was scare the wits out of her, apparently. He remembered the look on her face as she'd pulled the covers clear up to her chin. She had that city-worn, wary look about her—definitely the suspicious type. And not *his* type at all, he reminded himself for the hundredth time. Her little day trip from Washington seemed to have completely done her in, witnessed by the fact that she was sleeping so late this morning. Yes, she was definitely another Mary Lynn Baskin. Or was she?

He walked slowly toward the side door that led to the kitchen and caught his mother's voice as he mounted the steps to the entrance. When he heard Katherine Henry say his name, he nearly jumped out of his skin.

"Homer?" His mother was replying to Miss Henry's question. "He's our youngest. Of course, you'd never know it from looking at him, he's so tall. Taller than me—he's the only one who is. But I think he's the most handsome of all my children.''

Even as Homer felt like sinking into the ground, he strained to hear if Katherine Henry agreed with his mother. Unfortunately Ellie was already going on to describe the various heights and ages of his other siblings—Lacy, Tom, Ed and Oscar.

Soon, Homer noticed, Katherine Henry again brought the conversation back to him. So she was interested in him. Or rather, she was probably trying to glean all the information on him she could for that toy company.

"Oh, Homer loves living in Ludlum. Of course, he treats this more like his home base, with the paper and all. He's always been more of a wanderer than the others, always looking for new people to talk to, stories for his paper and the like. He's got a real knack with people, I think. And then he invents things like his armadillo trap to sell through mail order…''

Homer took two steps back, not at all pleased with the way his mother was presenting him to Katherine Henry. He wasn't sure why his mother's description disturbed him. He just didn't like that city woman poking around his life, he guessed. And his mother could have mentioned what a good job he had done revamping the paper, or how generous he was with his nieces and nephews; instead, she had practically made him sound like a hobo!

Before he could pull himself together, Katherine and his mother came out the door not two feet away from him.

"Homer!" his mother exclaimed. "What were you doing out here? Eavesdropping?"

"Of course not," Homer snapped back. He couldn't take his eyes off Katherine, who was dressed in one of

Lacy's old dresses. It was rose in color, and loose, making her look slimmer than ever, almost fragile.

She looked at him, too, but a little differently, as if he were some strange creature she didn't want to get too close to. He had thought she would be a little more at ease today, after having a good night's sleep, but if anything she seemed more jittery than ever.

Homer could only guess that she thought his clothes were all wrong. Before he could temper his words, he said, "What did you expect? Overalls?"

"Overalls?" she repeated, apparently giving the question serious thought, as though she hadn't heard the sarcasm lacing his words. She took in his charcoal tweed jacket and khaki trousers. "No, what you're wearing is fine."

She picked up her briefcase and edged by him on the small brick porch, following his mother out to the car. Restless to start the journey, Homer was close on their heels. When he reached her rental car, Ellie was handing Katherine a picnic basket and urging her to come to Ludlum again soon for a visit.

Fat chance, Homer thought.

*Another vagabond.*

Katherine had become suspicious when the two old men at the Ludlum Gas and Grocery said that Homer Ludlum was rarely in town. Then Ellie had confirmed her suspicions over breakfast. Even in the eyes of his own mother, the man had a bad case of wanderlust.

Katherine didn't know why it should bother her, but it did. Maybe because it reminded her of her mother just when she had finally put that part of her life behind her. She couldn't think of any other reason Homer Ludlum's way of life should affect her one way or the other.

But suddenly, Katherine couldn't wait to be back in Washington in the apartment she had lived in for four years without incident, back with her practically immovable thirty-gallon fish tank, her responsibility for Homer Ludlum over with.

One more day. All she had to do was deliver the man to Bill Warren, listen to what everybody had to say about the reversible latch, which couldn't be much, and then make sure Ludlum made it back to the airport in one piece.

But at the rate they were going, she was afraid she might never make it to Washington. She had allowed Homer to drive, thinking it would speed things up to have someone at the wheel who knew the way. That was her first mistake.

Once in the driver's seat, Homer had taken charge. The radio had been snapped on immediately, the air-conditioning turned off and the windows rolled down from the switches at his elbow. What was designed to be the ultimate in plush, comfortable driving suddenly became a hot, noisy wind tunnel.

"I love road trips, don't you?"

He sounded jubilant. Out of the corner of her eye, Katherine glimpsed a warm, generous smile she couldn't help returning, however briefly.

"Don't you think it's a little hot, Mr. Ludlum?" she asked.

"This? This is only April. Take off your coat," he urged. "And I think you can call me Homer."

Katherine did as he said, discovering she was comfortable enough. She had put on her raincoat as a sort of protective shield, but if they were going to drive alfresco, she was better off without it.

"You can call me Katherine," she said over the radio. She had to flatten the bodice of Lacy's too-big dress, which puffed out each time the wind caught it.

"Better, Katherine?" he asked, noticing she was now coatless.

"Great," she said automatically. Just one more day, she added to herself. She felt like a moron, having to clutch at her chest.

Homer sensed her agitation, but couldn't identify the source. "Don't you like easy-listening music?"

"That's fine with me," Katherine said, beginning to regret her decision to let this maniac behind the wheel. More annoying than the overly soothing music were his legs, which were so long they seemed to splay over to her side of the seat. She didn't want to think of what the plane ride would be like.

"I enjoy this kind of music because I can sing along," he explained, turning up Neil Sedaka a notch or two. Katherine sank a little lower in her seat as his booming baritone bellowed a verse of "Laughter in the Rain."

"Something wrong?"

"Not a thing," Katherine answered, feeling a smile tug at her lips.

He was also fond of detours. Already they had stopped by the side of the road to shoo some stray cows back into their pasture; then of course they had to drive over to the house of Woodie Ludlum, Homer's third cousin, to tell him the cows were out. After that, Homer informed her he had to deliver some papers to a nursing home not too far out of their way.

The radio station had finished playing two Judy Collins songs back to back when Homer decided it was time for another detour.

"You're going to love this," he said.

From the start, Homer had promised to show her some sights along the way. But as time passed, and they seemed to have backtracked more than they had moved forward, Katherine became edgier and edgier. She could tell they were on the outskirts of a town by the number of small houses dotting the sides of the road.

"Don't you think we should stop for gas?" She didn't want a repeat of last night.

"We're still three-quarters full," Homer answered. He was surprised at her question, since they had filled up in Ludlum. From her words and her behavior—she was constantly fidgeting—it seemed Katherine thought they'd been on the road for an eternity.

In truth, Katherine hated detours and would rather sit in a smelly filling station than be force-fed local color. She had taken enough detours in her first eighteen years to last her a lifetime. *And they had to get to Washington.* But that matter didn't seem to faze Homer. He bounced the Chevy down an unpaved rutted road, inadvertently jostling and bumping their legs together in the small front seat.

When the car came to a stop next to a small stone well, Katherine bounded out of the car and walked toward the waist-high structure. Water bubbled out of a small hole in the stones.

"Ever had real artesian well water?" Homer asked, coming up behind her.

"No," she answered. Texas was at least ten degrees hotter than Washington in April, however, and just looking at the clear water made her thirsty.

Homer produced a glass jar and, after filling it up, offered her a swig. She drank down half the contents.

"I bet it's not like the bottled kind you're used to," Homer said abruptly.

Katherine shook her head. "I don't have money to throw away on water. I take my chances with the tap, rusty pipes and all."

His brow wrinkled. "You shouldn't drink rusty water."

Katherine liked the timbre of his voice. It was deep, with a hint of a drawl she hadn't noticed at first. "Well, it's not really rusty," she answered with a faint laugh. "Just a little cloudy."

Homer glanced away, looking much like he had in the picture on Lacy's bedside table. "Shouldn't drink cloudy water, either," he said.

He offered her some more water, looking deeply into her eyes this time. She was adjusting to his height, and she liked the solidity that emanated from him. Normally she would be very anxious about getting somewhere on time, but here with Homer, she felt perfectly comfortable taking it easy and leaning against the well for a while, just enjoying the open air.

Homer shared her sentiments, although he was more enchanted by Katherine than the atmosphere. Her windblown hair looked fresh and clean in the sunshine, fresh and clean and touchable. He wished he could push one of the wisps back behind her ear. More than that, though, he wished he could find some way to ensure he would have a chance to get to know Katherine, to figure her out.

He didn't know what to expect once they got to Washington. Most likely he would be installed in some sterile hotel room, then trotted out when the toy-company executives were ready to give him their pitch. He had the feeling Katherine wouldn't be involved much after today.

That thought made him a little panicky. It meant that the most intriguing part of the trip was almost over. Unless . . .

"I've got an idea," he said suddenly.

Katherine looked up, squinting slightly in the sun. She appeared languid and relaxed. Receptive. "What's that?" she asked, smiling.

"Why don't we drive?" Homer asked.

Apparently that was the wrong thing to say. Katherine's jaw dropped open. She looked terrified. "Drive?" she asked. "To Washington?" Her tone made it sound as if he had suggested they drive to the moon.

"I thought it might be more fun than flying."

She continued to gape at him. "Fun?" she asked, stunned. "Fun? Mr. Ludlum, this is not a pleasure trip—I mean, Patriot Games and Toys wants you to enjoy yourself, certainly, but . . ."

Katherine's words trailed off as she appeared to be searching frantically for a way to deny his request. "I'm not authorized to drive," she said finally.

"You don't have a license?" Homer asked.

Katherine reddened. "I'm a company man, Mr. Ludlum. When Patriot says fly, I fly. I'm sorry." She looked at her watch. "And really, we should be going, or we'll never make the afternoon plane."

She pushed away from the well and walked briskly back to the car. Homer wasn't quite sure what to make of what had just happened as he ambled after her. Apparently he had hooked up with a true, by-the-book company person.

But as they continued on their journey, he began to suspect maybe the explanation wasn't as simple as that. He drove straight on, knowing how anxious she was to reach the airport, but every once in a while, he would weave a little to show Katherine points of interest along the way. Although she tried her best to hide it, he could tell she was interested in the historical markers and cemeteries and the world's largest flea market that he pointed out to her.

He just couldn't figure out why she thought she needed to submerge her curiosity about those things. Or why, when Harry Belafonte came on the radio when they were swinging through Dallas, she just didn't go ahead and sing along. Her tapping toes and bobbing head clearly indicated she wanted to.

She was never going to get on another airplane as long as she lived. Ever.

The checkered cab was barreling down the Dulles access road toward Washington, but Homer didn't seem to mind. He hadn't cared when they were bumped from two flights, either, stranded at Dallas-Fort Worth airport for hours. He liked airport coffee shops, he'd told Katherine. And not so he could flop into a comfortable booth, either. Homer Ludlum liked to sit at the counter, on those back-breaking stools, so he could chat with other stranded, demoralized airline passengers.

"This was Robert E. Lee's house before the Civil War," Katherine said now, watching Homer practically hang out the window as they passed Arlington National Cemetery. Arlington House was lighted beautifully from its perch on the hill, but Katherine was too stiff from the plane ride to get very excited about it.

"I thought so," Homer answered with unveiled enthusiasm. The man even approached cab rides with gusto.

Even in her exhaustion, she smiled. She could afford to be affable now, Katherine decided, since she was about to be rid of the man. It was doubtful that Bill Warren had allotted Homer much free time for sight-seeing, which was a shame. A man who got as excited as Homer did over artesian wells and flea markets would be over the moon at the Washington Monument.

"I hope you brought your camera," she said.

"Don't need one," Homer replied, thumping his temple with his forefinger. "Like to store it all up here. A memory's more durable than a photograph."

Katherine had the good grace to turn away before she rolled her eyes. Every time she began to feel kindly toward Homer, something he would do or say always brought her up short. The man seemed more like a lunatic the longer she was with him. Which bothered her, because he was definitely attractive; she had felt that plainly as they had sat in the connected plastic airport terminal seats, waiting for all three of their planes to take off. After half a day there, she almost wished she had taken Homer up on the driving idea. Almost.

But Homer had been annoyingly patient, not even caring that the airline had overbooked their first two flights. When Katherine had begun to make a scene at the airline ticket counter, he had sped her away.

"How can this not bother you?" she'd asked, fuming.

"It's not that woman's fault," he answered evenly.

He clamped both hands firmly on her shoulders to calm her—a gesture that produced the exact opposite effect, although Katherine would have died before letting him know that. Then he led her to the gift shop, where he purchased a legal pad and a pen, telling her that they could sit right down and write the airline a letter of complaint.

"Brother, are you naive," she'd muttered, and proceeded to buy a newspaper. By the time she'd finished reading the funnies and taking several stabs at the crossword puzzle, Homer had finished not only a letter to the airline, but one to his congressman, as well.

Most aggravating of all, however, was his suitcase, which followed him everywhere. Homer had installed a motor with a remote control to his small bag, which worked much like the electric toy cars that Patriot sold. He had explained that motorized suitcases were the wave of the future, with more and more people on the go. He seemed to understand those people very well.

They were opposites, Katherine decided as she stared out the cab window, and it was just as well their affiliation would be a brief one. She looked forward to dropping him off at his hotel and going home. It was eleven-thirty; even after her deep sleep the night before, she was pooped.

She had called Mr. Warren from the Dallas-Fort Worth airport. He was furious that she was late, of course, but relieved that Homer Ludlum was coming. They would simply have to put the presentation off for a while, he said genially, advising her to make sure Ludlum got checked in.

But when they arrived at the hotel, the man at the front desk said he had no reservation for Homer Ludlum. Past the point of argument, Katherine merely nodded and smiled as the man told them there were no vacancies. It was Friday night during cherry-blossom season, he explained, and there was a dental-ethics convention in the hotel. In fact, the hotel was *over*booked.

"Looks like you'll get your money's worth out of that notepad," Katherine said as she hailed another cab for them. "You can write your congressman about this, too."

"Aren't you going to call your boss?" Homer asked.

"No," Katherine said, "I'm going home."

Homer gave her a quizzical look as she opened the cab door. "I've got a couch," she offered.

He smiled. "That sounds just fine." He assumed his gentlemanly duties and held her arm as she eased onto the springy seat of the taxi. He followed close behind, carefully closing the door as she gave the driver her address in the Adams-Morgan section of the city.

"It's not exactly Park Avenue," she warned.

Homer laughed and briefly touched her hand.

Katherine's mouth went bone-dry at his touch and suddenly every inch of her body was wide awake. Was she crazy? The invitation had just slipped out. Now she wondered exactly what she'd gotten herself into. She scooted farther away in the seat.

Still, when they reached her apartment building, Katherine felt she'd never been happier to be anywhere in her life. The colorless old building looked big and sturdy and welcoming. And tonight the rickety elevator, which usually frightened her, seemed to glide like a dream up to the seventh floor. The hall was vacuumed and clean, and for a moment, Katherine was glad to be able to repay Homer's family's hospitality.

But all those pleasant feelings vanished when she reached her apartment. As she leaned against the door to fish her keys out of her purse, the door fell open.

Katherine leapt back, grabbing Homer's arm and pulling him away. They both came to a thudding halt when they collided with the hallway wall opposite.

"What's wrong?" Homer asked.

Katherine kept her eyes glued on her doorway. "The door was open," she whispered. "I think somebody's broken into my apartment!"

"I'll call the police," Homer said.

Katherine pressed her fingers against his chest, pinning him to the wall as she leaned forward and peered down the hall. "Did you see anything moving inside my apartment?"

"I didn't have time. You attacked me before I had a chance."

Forgetting the potential danger looming not ten feet away, Katherine turned on Homer. "I did not attack you. There could be killers in there. A lot of murders start out just like this—as burglaries," she explained. "What if they heard us get off the elevator?"

"Katherine, they might have left already."

"Well, I'm not going to be the one to find out."

Homer stepped forward cautiously, listening carefully. "Did you leave your radio on?" he asked.

"No. What do you hear?"

"Well…it sounds sort of like 'doo-be-doo-be-doo,'" he said.

"Like a rap song?" Katherine immediately pictured the more troubling-looking kids in the neighborhood.

"No," Homer said flatly. "Like Frank Sinatra."

"You mean—"

"'Strangers in the Night,'" he elaborated. "I'm almost positive."

Her indignation rising, Katherine marched right past Homer. This had been a hell of a day, and being burgled by easy-listening thugs was about the last straw.

"Wait, Katherine, let me go first," Homer entreated.

"It's my apartment," she answered bravely, and threw the door open. But as she stepped inside, she was horrified by what she saw. Coming straight at her, skittering on the hardwood floors and slobbering up a storm, was a Great Dane puppy.

Katherine shrieked, hit the floor and was attacked. The drooling dog, faced with its first real intruder, pawed and licked and whined. Covering her face protectively only seemed to agitate the animal more.

"Oh! You're back!"

Katherine looked beyond the fur and saw Gladys Hobbs padding over in her nightgown to welcome her. The old lady's silver hair was mussed.

"Millie and I must have fallen asleep. I'd only come down to check on the fish, and then I turned on the stereo for a second. You know, Katherine, if you're going to be out of town, you really should leave a light on or the stereo going. You shouldn't be too trusting, not even of people in your own building."

Disappointed she hadn't found a burglar, Millie scrambled over to greet Homer. Katherine picked herself up off the floor.

Seeing Homer herself, Mrs. Hobbs gave an extra-big smile and said, "I got your note, Katherine. I didn't know you were going to be gone for *two* days, though. Nevertheless, I didn't hear you come in, and I know you pamper those fish, feeding them twice a day like you do. Of course, if I'd known you were bringing a friend home..." Her voice trailed off in a thinly disguised request for an introduction.

"Mrs. Hobbs, this is Homer Ludlum, from Texas. Homer, Gladys Hobbs, from upstairs." She said it mechanically, picked up the remote to Homer's luggage and headed farther in to the apartment, followed by the suitcase. Homer and Gladys exchanged pleasantries by the doorway.

They were still chatting when Katherine came back from the kitchen, where she had started heating water. She rarely entertained people, but she supposed she should offer her guests something. "Would you like some tea, Mrs. Hobbs?" she asked.

"Oh, thank you," the elderly woman twittered. "I love hot tea before bed."

Back in the kitchen, Katherine listened to them gabbing like old friends. She felt invaded. When she returned to the living room with a steaming pot of Earl Grey tea, the conversation had switched from the climate of the Southwest to air safety, and her two visitors were comfortably seated on the couch. Homer was telling Mrs. Hobbs that, in the air force jets, seats faced backward. Mrs. Hobbs was saying that made a lot of sense to her. And Millie was thumping her tail happily on the rug in front of the coffee table.

Katherine sipped her tea and looked at Homer. He appeared relaxed in her living room, as though he was meant to be there. And he seemed to genuinely enjoy talking to Mrs. Hobbs, whereas Katherine had never paid much attention to her neighbor before, except as a handy person in the building she could turn to during crises.

She began to rethink her day with Homer. He was a hopeless vagabond like her mother. But unlike Marge Henry, Homer seemed to thrive on the experience of being on the go. With her mother, moving around had been a kind of obsession, as though she didn't know what she was looking for and was quickly disenchanted with whatever she found. But Homer seemed happy to take things and people as they came.

Still, Katherine found it unnatural. If she owned a business, she would never leave it, especially one she was as dedicated to as Homer seemed to be to the *Ludlum Free Press*. He'd never been married, his mother had told her that morning. Katherine also found that fact interesting. Homer appeared to be in his early thirties. But then, there probably weren't many young women in a town like Ludlum. At least she hadn't seen any.

When her eyes met his steely blue ones, Katherine pulled her gaze away. Why was she worrying about whether he was married or not? What Homer Ludlum did with his life was none of her concern. What's more, their shared glance had sent a tingle up her spine, and she didn't like that at all. She began to regret more than ever that the hotel didn't have a vacancy.

Homer straightened instinctively, trying to concentrate on Gladys Hobbs's words, which was difficult with Katherine there. It was strange to see Katherine in what he supposed were her natural surroundings. There wasn't much in the room to suggest her personality. The small living room was bright, with lightly varnished furniture and white walls, but aside from two tiny goldfish in a huge bare tank, the room was rather impersonal.

He'd been elated when Katherine offered him shelter for the night. But if he was really going to get an opportunity to know her better, it would have to be through talking to her, not by what he could glean from her habitat. First, though, he would have to get rid of the neighbor, nice as she was. He began dropping hints about what a long day he and Katherine had had.

Katherine was surprised that Gladys didn't stay much longer. As Homer walked the woman to the door, Katherine stretched and suppressed a deep yawn, listening to their warm parting, which made them sound as if they were longtime chums. Gladys called for her dog and, almost as an afterthought, said, "Good night, Katherine."

"Good night," Katherine called back, flopping back into her chair. When she heard Homer flip the dead bolt and fasten the chain, she sat up immediately. With those two noises, the apartment suddenly became smaller, more intimate. Too intimate.

"You look beat," Homer said, standing in the middle of the room a few feet from her.

"I am tired," Katherine replied, trying to think of the fastest, most efficient way to pull out the sleeper couch and retreat to her room.

Homer chuckled softly and plopped on the couch with a sigh. "You don't seem to travel well," he offered tentatively.

"I guess I'm a homebody," Katherine explained. She certainly couldn't pull out the couch with him on it. "I don't like to be on the road."

"I do," he said.

"I know. Your mother told me all about you."

He knew it! Homer wondered what else his mother had told her. "You can't always trust mothers not to, uh, twist things."

Katherine nodded. Was *that* the truth, she thought, temporarily distracted from the task of getting them to bed. Her own mother thought Katherine was as dull as dishwater. Marge had always treated her as though she was her cross to bear.

Homer leaned forward. "Why don't you like to travel, Katherine?" he asked softly. Her expression was pensive, sad, and he wondered what memories lay behind those honey-brown eyes that could cause such a melancholy look.

Katherine was drawn to Homer's lazy, understanding gaze. He had a trustworthy face, she decided, but she fought against revealing herself to a virtual stranger.

"When you move around, you lose things," she said, her voice sounding quivery even to her own ears, and she looked toward him to see if he had noticed.

His lips formed a slight smile, and he looked virile and adorable and knowing all at once. "But sometimes," he said huskily, "you can find things, too."

"That's never happened to me," Katherine said. A stray lock of brown hair fell across his brow, and she had to suppress the urge to lean over and smooth it back. She shook her head. It was definitely time to put this day to rest.

She was shutting him out again, and Homer knew it. He hoped he would get the chance to speak to her again during his stay in Washington. Of course, he couldn't tell her he really had no interest in her corporation, only her. Knowing Katherine even as little as he did, he knew she would somehow take offense. Telling her he was more interested in her more as a woman than as an employee of Patriot Games and Toys would probably scare the hell out of her. But, he realized, that was the way he'd felt about her from the moment he saw her walking along the blacktop road into Ludlum.

"You look tired," he said again, giving her the chance to take her leave.

"Yes, I am," Katherine said eagerly, then realized she might have sounded a bit rude. "Actually, I'm not half as tired as I usually am. Last night was the first night I've really slept in over a month."

She smiled, recalling how peaceful it had been in East Texas, how silent. Then she looked at Homer's pleased expression and remembered their stilted conversation of the night before. She hoped he didn't think she'd slept well because of him....

"You see, something good did come of your excursion," Homer said.

"I just need to invest in some earplugs," Katherine said, "so I can learn to sleep as well in my own bed as I did in yours."

That hadn't come out right, and Katherine knew it the minute she said it. Homer rubbed his chin speculatively, a wicked glint playing in his eyes.

"I mean—" She broke off and stood up. "Well, you know what I mean. I'm afraid I'm going to have to be a bad hostess and turn in."

Homer was obviously tired, too, because he didn't even seem to register her words.

"I'll bring you some blankets and things. The couch folds out," she added a little more loudly.

Homer looked up at her, smiling politely, almost seeming to dismiss her from the room. The man had a lot of gall, Katherine thought as she headed for the linen closet in the bathroom. First he mesmerized her with those blue eyes of his into saying all sorts of private things she didn't want to say, then he completely tuned her out.

She should have been glad, though. Her thoughts had been moving in disturbing directions back there in the living room. She wondered how many women before her had been captivated by Homer's lazily seductive style, and tried to imagine every house in Ludlum as one in which Homer had left a heartbroken woman. The thought sobered her a little.

Homer Ludlum was just another vagabond passing through her life. He was worse than her mother, even.

The man obviously couldn't even keep his mind from wandering.

But then, neither could she. She dreaded trying to go to sleep. Not only was it a Friday—almost always the loudest night of the week—but she definitely felt odd having a man in the place. She hadn't grown up around men, so she didn't really know what to expect. She hoped Homer had brought pajamas with him.

A fleeting mental image stopped her dead in her tracks. Clutching a set of floral sheets to her chest, she stood in her tiny hallway and winced at the thought of a chance middle-of-the-night encounter with a very exposed Homer Ludlum. But that was silly, she decided. A person named Homer was sure to sleep in more than his shorts.

Any reservations she had about their sleeping arrangements vanished as she walked into the living room on slightly wobbly legs. Homer, busy folding out the couch, barely acknowledged her as she came in and set the linens down. Then, when he opened his suitcase and pulled out a neatly folded pair of brown cotton pajamas printed with tiny blue diamonds, it was like a slap on the face.

Not that she'd expected him to flash his bedroom eyes and seduce her right there on her own fold-out couch. She certainly didn't think of Homer Ludlum in that way, and she had only met him yesterday, after all. But it wasn't exactly flattering to be ignored, either. Not in the least, she seethed, fetching a pillow.

She plopped it down next to where he was sitting—on the bed—and cleared her throat.

"Good night, then," she said.

"Night," he muttered absently.

Fifteen minutes later, safely encased in the highest necked, starchiest nightgown she owned, Katherine tucked herself in under three layers of covers and turned out the light.

On cue, the sounds of the Washington night engulfed her. Horns wailed, boom boxes boomed, sirens screeched, and it seemed that every car with a broken tailpipe had chosen tonight to cruise down her street. Millie began her nightly ritual on the floor above, yowling and prancing with her big puppy paws right above Katherine's head. But even more distracting than all of those noises was the mere idea of Homer, in brown-and-blue pajamas, just on the other side of her door.

As if in answer to her thoughts, she heard the radio in the living room click on, followed by an instrumental version of an old Peter, Paul and Mary song. Seconds later, when Homer's mellow baritone began crooning "Puff, the Magic Dragon," it was almost more than she could bear.

Her first thought was to stomp out there and give the man a piece of her mind, but remembering that she was in her gown, no matter how grannyish, she thought better of that plan. Instead, she flipped over onto her stomach, her head sandwiched between two feather pillows.

She didn't hear the knock at the door. Only the slightest of depressions on her mattress told her she wasn't the only person in her bed anymore. She bolted upright and came nose to nose with Homer.

"What are you doing in here?" she yelped, flicking on the nightstand lamp.

"You looked like you needed a sandman."

"What kind of man?" she asked, shocked.

"A sandman," he said again. He held up both hands, each holding pieces of material.

"Homer," Katherine said firmly, "what am I supposed to do with those?"

"Sleep," he replied.

To her dismay, he edged a little closer, his thigh brushing against hers. She could barely concentrate on the little wads of cloth Homer was so exuberantly showing her.

He put one of the things aside and started his demonstration. "Now what I did was take one of your shower caps—I hope you don't mind, I saw you had an extra—and rip out the elastic." He rapidly stretched the material to illustrate. "Then all I had to do was snip the toes off a pair of my socks, stuff them with cotton, then sew it all together. And there you have it."

"What do I have?"

Homer knitted his brows together. "Didn't you say you were going to invest in some earplugs?"

The purpose of his invention finally dawned on her. "You mean you want me to put your socks on my ears?" she squeaked.

Homer frowned. "They're clean. And it's much more efficient than just sticking a plug in your ear that's going to fall out the minute you roll over. This way, the elastic keeps them secure."

"Why are you doing this?" she asked.

He gently cupped her ear and slipped the material around it. It was a snug fit, she had to admit.

"You said you couldn't sleep," he said. He retracted his leg, apparently sensing some impropriety on his part.

Katherine felt like a heel for not receiving his gift more enthusiastically. And her leg was homesick for his immediately. She tilted her muffled ear toward the window and realized she could hear things, but only through her other ear. "I think it's working," she said.

Homer nodded. "Cotton is the best insulation." He proceeded to wrap her other ear as carefully as he had the first. This time, she was acutely aware of his palm as it gently brushed her temple. When one of his roughened fingertips hesitated at her earlobe, she nearly popped out of her skin.

He pulled away then to survey his creation, and Katherine watched him through a cocoon of quiet. But the blood rushing through her veins en route to every pressure point in her body soon filled the vacuum; her heartbeat seemed to be thundering in her ears. A person could go crazy with no noise, she realized.

She half expected Homer to yank the things off her ears at any moment and clinically go about making improvements. But as always, he did what she least expected.

Taking each of her arms in a firm grip, he gently pressed her down until she was flat on her back. If she was going to protest, this was the time to do it, she knew. But she didn't resist. Almost in a dream state, her whole body betrayed her. She felt an airy tingling in her limbs, a quickening of her pulse, and she closed her eyes. When his hands smoothed down her hair, she thought for sure he would see her entire being shudder, even through three layers of covers.

When she opened her eyes again, he was nowhere in sight. He had turned out the light, though, and left her to contemplate what had just happened, or hadn't happened, between them. In silence.

Homer came out of Katherine's bedroom like a drowning man gasping for air. He should never have

gone in there in the first place, he told himself. His best
intentions had definitely gone awry.

It had taken all the willpower he had not to crawl right
under those covers with her. Which would have been a
terrible mistake. Katherine's attitude all day had made
it clear how she felt about him; she obviously thought he
was a naive simpleton, an absentminded inventor from
the middle of nowhere. That her body had been tele-
graphing the opposite message helped neither of them.

Something—or more likely, someone—had drained all
the adventure right out of her spirit. He had never met
a more staid, root-bound person in his life. The woman
even read the comics like an accountant would the fi-
nancial pages. She had that same manic seriousness.
Slipping between the sheets on the pull-out couch, he
tried to envision Katherine as a kid. But Katherine
Henry skipping rope was a hard thing to imagine. The
woman he had come to know in the past day looked as
if she'd been born an adult.

But mostly, he couldn't envision her as a child because his memory was clogged with the vision of her all
grown up, lying in bed with her eyes closed. Just on the
other side of that door.

Even with his socks on her ears, she was sexy as hell.
Even wearing that awful flannel nightgown that swallowed her beautiful figure, she was cool and feminine—
and damned desirable. And even knowing they had
about as much in common as a Persian kitten and a pack
mule didn't stop his libido from galloping way ahead of
his reason.

A lot of people had come to Ludlum hoping to lure
him into a contract. She even looked like them all, only
feminine. Business suit, medium heels, severe bun. And
no life.

But while most of them showed a lot of fake enthusiasm over a harmless trap for animals that dug holes everywhere, Katherine had not. Clearly, she was the wrong person to lure anybody to the city. But that was just what made him want to go. She was the unexpected, a walking contradiction—the reluctant emissary, a woman who had been places but had prematurely hit inertia.

She said she was afraid of losing things. But Homer had never lost anything—he just kept finding and finding. And if he had stayed home with the paper, he would never have discovered Katherine. Now he wanted to get to know the *real* Katherine.

He had seen her foot tapping to the easy-listening music she would only admit to just tolerating. And although she would never admit it, she had come very close to jumping out of the car when they passed that flea market. He had even made her laugh once, although he couldn't remember exactly when.... Ah, yes. The water. She had laughed about having rusty, or cloudy, water. Nobody as rigid as she pretended to be could have laughed about that.

He was definitely going to check her out and see what else could bring a smile to her face. And he prayed that maybe, just maybe, he could infuse a little joy into the determinedly dour Miss Henry. He didn't know how much time he had. But then, he could always be inventive when something important was at stake.

He would start by investigating her pipes.

## Chapter Three

At first Katherine thought she was dreaming. Her eyes were open, but the noise that had awakened her had a muted, faraway quality to it. Only when she flopped over onto her side to try to go to sleep again did she feel the cotton against her ears and remember Homer's late-night visit. Then she recognized the noise as the muffled sound of her telephone ringing not two feet away.

She reached to the nightstand and picked up the receiver, ripping the sock contraption off her ear at the same time. "Hello?"

"Henry! I've been trying to get you all morning. Where have you been for Pete's sake?"

Bill Warren's bark didn't register for a moment as Katherine indulged in a half-somnolent, self-satisfied moment of peace. Two nights of sleep in a row. She had never slept so well before she met Homer Ludlum. Then she remembered the man himself, and that brought mixed feelings she wasn't ready to deal with, at least not before she'd had her first cup of coffee and a look at the comics.

"I'm sorry, Mr. Warren. What were you saying?"

"I'm saying, what have you done with Homer Ludlum?" His tone brooked no nonsense.

But then, Bill Warren wasn't exactly the wronged party in this instance, Katherine thought, not forgetting some of the more disturbing, frustrating moments of the day before.

"He's here," she answered brusquely.

"There? At your apartment?" Warren's tone shifted dramatically from the acerbic to the salacious.

"On my couch," Katherine fumed. "There was a little trouble with the hotel room—"

"Didn't I give you the name of the hotel?"

"You gave me the name of *a* hotel. They said they had no reservation for Homer Ludlum."

"Well, as long as he's safe," Warren said, dismissing the many unspoken questions Katherine was mentally hurling across the telephone wire. "I probably gave you the wrong address or something."

"Yes, probably," Katherine agreed suspiciously.

"So, what's this Ludlum like?"

Katherine hesitated. *He sings to the radio and actually writes his congressman. He talks to strangers as though they were longtime chums. He invents things to make me sleep better.* There were a number of ways to answer her boss's question, but none would be the response he was looking for.

"Intriguing," she said finally.

"Intriguing? What does that mean?"

"Homer Ludlum's not somebody you can pin down very easily, Mr. Warren. He's enigmatic."

"You mean he's got a few screws loose."

Katherine sighed. She didn't like the sound of his description, but maybe it was apt. Maybe she was beginning to let Homer's kinder qualities get to her. She was forgetting that at heart he was really a vagabond. And most important, she was forgetting her job. Homer Ludlum had one purpose in her life—he was an assignment, no different than the many memos she typed up daily and deposited on Warren's desk.

No different, she thought, except that he had sexy blue eyes that could make her knees quiver, and a deep voice that, when not singing Barry Manilow songs, practically sent her into a swoon. But recognizing the folly of her wayward feelings gave her control over them. From now on, it was back to business as far as Homer Ludlum was concerned.

"I don't think we'll have any problems with him," she told her boss. "He's a bit scattered, but harmless." Harmless. The word rang false even as she said it.

"That's good. Any other problems?"

"Not really. When do you want to see him?"

"Be sure he's in my office at nine on Monday."

"Monday!" It was only Saturday, and the words of the man at the hotel front desk came back to her with stunning clarity. "But it's cherry-blossom season, and there's a dental-ethics convention in town," she said. "Where am I supposed to put him?"

"What's the matter with keeping him where he is?"

More was the matter with that than she could ever admit to her employer. "He's sleeping on my couch. It's not exactly what I promised when I dragged him all the way up here." As though Homer Ludlum had to be *dragged* anywhere, she thought.

"You've got a point, Henry. I was thinking we might do the shareholders a favor, but what you say makes sense."

That didn't sit well with Katherine, either. Warren always made it very clear that when the shareholders were put out, their discomfort trickled straight down to the consumer. Corporate guilt weighed heavily upon her.

"I'm sure it's not that big a deal, Mr. Warren. He seems fairly easygoing." That was the understatement of the century. If Homer Ludlum were any more easygoing, he'd probably go right off the planet.

"I'll call around and get back to you." Warren seemed to be weighing the alternatives. "In the meantime, try to keep him happy."

The phrase brought fresh panic. "Happy?" she squeaked. "How? What am I supposed to do?"

"Do whatever he wants to do, Henry."

That was just the answer she'd feared. "I'll take him sight-seeing," she offered.

"Good idea. Henry, you're a brick."

After Bill Warren had hung up, Katherine felt as if she had lost her lifeline. What on earth was she going to do now? She dreaded getting up, wanted to put off for as long as she could giving Homer the news he'd be staying with her. For one thing, she didn't know how he would react. Would he be glad of the opportunity to stay with her? Or was he as uncomfortable with the physical attraction between them as she was? Or worse still, maybe he wasn't aware of it at all....

Assuring herself she wouldn't be visible from the living room, she darted across the hall from the bedroom to the bathroom. The small, tiled room felt different, smelled different. A bottle of after-shave gave evidence of a living masculine presence—an alien presence to

Katherine. She picked up the bottle carefully and inspected it, conscious that she was snooping. She began to unscrew the bottle's black cap, then thought better of it. The after-shave was in the air already, and it would be masochistic to want it to be any more pungent. She put the bottle away quickly.

Her gaze alighted on a stranger sight. She gasped, then realized the contraption she was looking at must be Homer's toothbrush. He had fashioned it out of a hypodermic needle, but he had replaced the needle with bristles. The tube itself held toothpaste—the tricolored striped variety—which was pushed through to the head with the plunger.

Gaping, it dawned on her that this little item was an all-in-one toothbrush and toothpaste dispenser produced from Homer's imagination. Like all his inventions she had seen, it was so odd-looking that it would have appeared harebrained if it weren't so practical. The man obviously had a knack for solving life's little difficulties.

She was tempted to squeeze the plunger and watch the toothpaste ooze through the bristles. She couldn't actually do that of course; it wasn't *her* all-in-one toothbrush. But like the urge to scratch a mosquito bite, the itch to push that little plastic plunger grew stronger and stronger as she washed her face, then stronger yet as she brushed her teeth with her own dull toothbrush.

She looked at her watch and saw that it was already ten-thirty. Surely it wasn't too early to check on her guest. She wanted to tell him how clever she thought this latest invention was. After throwing on jeans and a T-shirt, she approached the living room cautiously.

But Homer wasn't in the living room, or anywhere else that she could see. The couch was made up, the sheets, blankets and pillow piled tidily on the chair. Flying to the kitchen, she noticed the tea things from last night washed and stacked neatly on the drying rack.

She turned on her heel and doubled back to the main room, hoping against all reason that she had somehow overlooked him. But missing Homer's six-foot frame in her tiny apartment would be pretty difficult, she admitted as she peered around the room, getting more panicky by the second.

The sound of paws hitting the floor above calmed her a little. Of course. She had mentioned that Mrs. Hobbs lived upstairs. Homer had probably gotten restless and taken it into his head to visit his new friend. At least, that's what Katherine rationalized on the ride up in the elevator.

Gladys Hobbs practically bubbled over as she ushered Katherine into her apartment. It was identical in space, if not in decor, to her own. Mrs. Hobbs leaned heavily toward doilies and knickknacks, and the Great Dane looked decidedly out of place, like the proverbial bull in the china shop. Katherine reached down and patted the animal's head, all the while looking nervously about the room. Mrs. Hobbs chattered on about how nice her "young man" was, but so far hadn't given Katherine a clue as to his whereabouts.

"Have you seen Homer, Mrs. Hobbs?" Katherine asked, trying to keep the anxious tone out of her voice.

"Seen him!" Mrs. Hobbs replied. "Why, we had breakfast together. He's just the sweetest, most considerate man I've ever met. He said he'd been out exploring and had discovered a Greek delicatessen. Did you know there was one of those around here?"

"No," Katherine said. Homer obviously wasn't there. And he'd been out wandering—no telling where he had gone after he'd worn out the pavement in their neighborhood.

"I'm still not sure where it is. Homer admitted to having gone pretty far afield."

Katherine swallowed a big gulp of air and nodded. "When exactly was this?"

"Oh! Early," Mrs. Hobbs answered cheerily, apparently not noticing that a pint of blood had drained out of Katherine's face. "We had the baklava that he had found at the Greek deli. There's some left over, if you'd like a piece."

"No, thank you, Mrs. Hobbs. I really have to be going."

Mrs. Hobbs escorted her to the door. After saying their goodbyes, the older woman admonished, "Honey, you can just call me Gladys. Homer does."

Back on the elevator, Katherine collapsed against the wall. What was she going to do now? Homer could be anywhere. The key was not to panic. The elevator stopped on the fifth floor, and a short, elderly man with a mustache got on. He smiled politely at Katherine.

"You're Homer's friend, aren't you?" he asked.

The man's words were like a dousing with ice water. Had Homer introduced himself to every person in her building? "Yes . . . yes I am," she answered.

"Homer isn't back from the parade yet?"

Katherine straightened. "What parade?"

"Said he read in the paper that there was a parade today. Down Pennsylvania Avenue."

Katherine scanned her mental calendar, trying to peg what holiday people could possibly be celebrating. But Memorial Day was still a month away. Which meant she would just have to go to Pennsylvania Avenue and find out for herself.

"What time does it start?" she asked the man as the doors opened to the lobby.

"Homer didn't say a thing about what time."

She should have guessed. She inwardly cursed Homer Ludlum and his darned earplugs for making her sleep late. Then she added a brief hex on her boss for getting her into this situation in the first place. By the time she reached Pennsylvania Avenue, she'd mentally maligned practically everyone she'd ever met.

The wide sidewalk was chockablock with people. Katherine still didn't know what all the fuss was about, so she angled her way toward the street for a better view.

It was the craziest thing she'd ever seen. A mishmash of humanity was marching down the avenue without any particular rhyme or reason. A local senior citizens' club dressed in square-dance garb was bouncing down the street, followed by a group whose banner proudly proclaimed them the Precision Lawn Mower Drill Team. Katherine stood, her mouth agape, watching as a motley crew of citizens maneuvered their hand lawn mowers in perfectly synchronized patterns.

After they had passed, Katherine turned to the woman next to her and asked what the parade was in celebration of.

"It's the Gross National Parade." The woman shrugged. "It's just for the heck of it."

Leave it to Homer to find a parade with no purpose, she thought, again plunging into the sea of people on the sidewalk. She followed the procession as it turned onto M Street. When they reached the outskirts of Georgetown, Katherine decided her manhunt was futile. The Virginia Association of Beekeepers was passing by to the recorded strains of "The Flight of the Bumblebee." Katherine noticed a vacant bench outside a sportswear store and moved toward it. Once she was sitting, she began to relax a little. *It's no big deal,* she thought. *A man who would go to the trouble of inventing a reversible latch for an armadillo trap can surely find his way back to the apartment.*

For the first time, she noticed it was a beautiful spring day. She even began to enjoy watching the tail end of the beekeepers swarming down the street in their white suits and bizarre headgear. They certainly resembled bees. Katherine laughed softly, and then heard someone next to her on the bench sharing her mirth.

It was Homer.

"Enjoying yourself?" he asked.

Katherine was speechless. The man had nerve! Did he think she was just out for a Saturday stroll?

"I've been looking all over for you!" she exclaimed.

Homer frowned. "Didn't you get my note?"

"Note?" she asked, sinking a little on the bench.

His blue eyes were dark with concern. "I left you a note on the refrigerator. When I went back to the apartment, you were gone. I was worried."

He was worried. All of her righteous anger dissolved at the preposterousness of it all. "I didn't see it," she explained. "I was so nervous about losing Patriot's honored guest, I panicked."

*Patriot's honored guest.* Homer had forgotten all about that. Something in his heart plummeted. She was a dutiful employee through and through. Sometime soon he was going to have to explain to her that he didn't give a damn about her toy company or what they wanted to do with his latch. He couldn't imagine that a company as big as Patriot would need his seal of approval, anyway, patent or no patent.

Damn. He should have stayed put this morning. But one thing had led to another . . . He remembered the paper sack in his hand.

"I found a filter for your tap," he said.

"My what?" As usual, Katherine wasn't following him at all.

"Your water's cloudy. You needed a filter, so I got one." He pulled the small box containing the filter from the bag and presented it to her.

She looked at him as though he had two heads, then started reading the directions on the box. He wished she would say something. She turned the box over and read the company's blurb that proclaimed how wonderful their filter was. He was feeling more foolish by the second.

"I can't believe you did this," she said.

Her cheeks were red, and Homer guessed that she felt uncomfortable accepting such a personal gift from him. Not that it was personal, really, but he was beginning to understand that Katherine Henry had an exaggerated sense of privacy. "I just picked it up at the hardware store," he explained. The woman was turning him in circles. Suddenly he was embarrassed about having done what he'd thought was the only practical thing to do.

"I'm surprised you didn't just whip up something off the top of your head."

"Some things are better ready-made," he said simply.

Katherine brightened. "I can't wait to try it out. I'll have to pay you for it, though."

His gift was not going over the way he'd planned at all. He'd wanted to put her at ease, to thank her for letting him stay at her place for the night. But all he had done apparently was cause her a lot of trouble and make her beholden to him. And all over her damned tap water.

"It's nothing," he said.

"But I have to pay you for it," Katherine insisted.

He waved off her protest. "Why don't we discuss it over something to eat," he offered.

"Eat?" she asked nervously. "We really should be getting back, I think. Mr. Warren should be calling. He might have already."

"Your boss?" Homer asked. "What does he want?"

"You, of course."

Homer hesitated. "Warren wants to talk to me this weekend?"

Katherine rethought her words and knew she was losing her mind. Homer had her so muddled she wasn't thinking clearly. "He's trying to find a hotel for you."

"Oh."

"Is that okay?" Katherine questioned.

"What's the alternative?"

"My couch."

The glint she saw in Homer's eye sent another little tingle dancing up her spine. He obviously preferred staying at her place to an impersonal hotel room. Which was natural for Homer. Still, this discovery played to her weaker side, the side that actually wanted him to stay. Now that she'd found him, she didn't want to lose him again. Not only that, but she actually found herself looking forward to spending some time with Homer, if only for the afternoon. And hadn't Bill Warren asked her to show him the sights?

"I guess it would be okay to have lunch," she said evenly. "As long as we get back to check my answering machine sometime this afternoon."

"Great," Homer said. "Where to now?"

Katherine didn't know what to say. She wasn't a social butterfly by any stretch of the imagination. If Bill Warren had been aware of her limited knowledge of the city, he wouldn't have been half so enthusiastic about leaving Homer in her hands. "I don't really know anywhere in this neighborhood we could go for lunch," she hedged.

"I can't believe that," Homer said. "It's a beautiful area. Haven't you come here on a date before?"

Katherine stiffened. She could barely remember the last time she'd had anything resembling a date. But she didn't want to tell Homer that—not that it was any of his business, anyway. "I don't come to Georgetown very often," she said evasively.

Homer put his hand on top of hers. "Don't worry about that. I spotted the perfect place this morning."

Homer's idea of a perfect place was a spot on the grass beside the Lincoln Memorial where they could have a picnic. Katherine argued that they should consult the Yellow Pages for the name of a real restaurant nearby. She wasn't sure she wanted to sit on the grass with Homer Ludlum, but he was adamant, dragging her into a variety of stores to buy odds and ends for their meal.

"I have some tuna salad at my place we could whip into sandwiches," Katherine had protested. They could check her answering machine that way, too.

But he was having none of it, and by the time their cab dropped them off in front of the massive monument, they were loaded down with fruit, cheese, falafel and chocolate-chip cookies.

"I feel a little strange eating Middle Eastern food in front of the Lincoln Memorial," Katherine said as they spread the feast before them on the grass. Picnics had always seemed a bit too unstructured for her taste. But then, she'd only ever had picnics with Marge, and everything was unstructured with her mother.

"I think old Abe would be pleased," Homer said, offering Katherine an orange.

They talked easily after that, about Lincoln, the situation in the Middle East—or what they could make of it—and other current events. Katherine was surprised to discover that they were in agreement on most topics and even more surprised to find herself laughing and having a good time.

During a brief lull, she remembered Homer's toothbrush and expressed her admiration for it.

"I'm still working out the kinks on that one," Homer said.

"What's the matter with it?"

"Well," Homer explained, a grin tugging at his lips, "it's mighty hard to get that fancy striped toothpaste into those little bitty syringes."

Katherine laughed. "You'll just have to invent a new machine that'll do it for you."

Her laughter bowled him over. She looked incredibly beautiful today in just a T-shirt and jeans. Her long brown hair was loose for once, falling in unruly waves over her shoulders and sometimes blowing in wispy strands across her face. If he were an artist, he'd try to capture on canvas her beauty and this rare moment—the day, the monument and her smile. It was shy, as though she weren't used to it. And when she talked to him as easily as she had just now, words seemed to gush out of her.

"Or maybe you should just invent a bigger hypodermic," she continued, "like the real menacing kind you see on cartoons."

He laughed with her. "You seem pretty imaginative yourself," he said. "Maybe you should be the inventor."

Katherine shook her head, becoming her serious self again. "No, I'm afraid I'm not the type for discovering things. Some people are born leaders—I'm a born follower."

"I think you underestimate yourself," Homer replied, frowning.

"I'm just being realistic. And I like to help people. Not everyone can follow orders. If I'm successful at all, it's because I know my limitations."

Homer scooted closer to her. "Why do you insist on selling yourself short?"

Katherine looked up at him despite her better judgment. His face was inches from hers, his broad chest a solid wall next to her. He seemed to be studying her, inch by inch, his cool blue eyes blazing a trail across her forehead, down the bridge of her nose, hovering at her lips. Slowly his large hand made its way to the tender area beneath her chin. She sucked in a breath, but her lungs felt as though they'd collapsed. She couldn't summon a muscle to move her to safety, couldn't grab enough air into her body to protest what she knew was coming.

His lips brushed hers softly, fleetingly, then he pulled them away again, his gaze fixed on hers. She thought perhaps he had changed his mind about kissing her, but that was before she felt his hands closing over her shoulders, taking her into his grasp. He launched a whole new assault, one she was totally unprepared for.

His mouth came down on hers firmly this time, almost roughly, his tongue toying with her rigid lower lip. Sensations raced through her, her lower body churning with unfamiliar feelings that spread like darts through her limbs. She instinctively curved a strangely heavy arm to his chest, which then seemed to snake of its own accord to the back of Homer's neck. She felt the tip of her tongue touch his, and her whole being was singed by the heat of the contact.

She shouldn't be kissing Homer Ludlum, she told herself as she angled her head to receive the warmth of his mouth more deeply. She barely knew him. What she did know indicated they were completely incompatible. Worse still, kissing Homer Ludlum was thoroughly unprofessional behavior.

Still, she had never felt anything like this before, and her instinct was simply to melt away in the comfort of the strong arms holding her. A gravelly moan reached her ears, and to her distress, she realized it had come out of her own throat.

She yanked her head abruptly away from his. The first things she saw were the empty bags that had held their lunch. She reached for one and started clearing up the leftovers, but Homer held her arm firmly, making the task impossible, forcing her to look at him squarely. She complied, warning herself not to lose her head again.

"We need to get back," Katherine sputtered. "Mr. Warren has probably called already."

"I think I know what you need, Katherine," Homer said, his husky voice making her stomach feel like a blender set on puree. But once his suggestive comment registered, it struck her as unforgivably presumptuous.

She jerked out of his grasp and bolted to her feet. Homer followed, and she turned on him. "I don't think one kiss allows you to dictate what I need."

This was what came from kissing people you didn't know too well, Katherine scolded herself. They could turn on the charm for two days and then transform into wolves the minute you let down your guard.

He took her hand in his gently. "It's what we both need. Come with me."

"Where?" she asked, bracing herself for a lurid answer.

"To see Hsing-Hsing."

Katherine's jaw involuntarily dropped. "What's that?"

"The panda at the National Zoo."

By the time they reached the panda cage, Katherine's legs ached from hiking up the steep inclines of the zoo. But she appreciated the park's natural layout for the animals' sakes. Zoos had always seemed sad places to her as a child, with their cramped cages and unhappy, penned animals. But the National Zoo was a treasure. The layout was spacious, and the pens were designed to resemble the animals' natural habitats as closely as possible.

Homer had insisted on seeing everything from pumas to prairie dogs. Katherine had tried to convince him during the entire subway ride over that they could easily stop by her apartment, check her answering machine and maybe see if Mrs. Hobbs wanted to join them. Homer had resisted her ideas, especially the last. But his enthusiasm for the animals eventually put Katherine at ease. She almost forgot about their kiss at the Lincoln Memorial—almost.

Hsing-Hsing, China's gift to the American people, was almost invisible, napping behind a log in the rear of his woodsy den. But visitors clamored around the fence, pointing and watching as if the animal was performing tricks, instead of sleeping. Katherine and Homer jockeyed for a good view and were duly awed by what they could see of the exotic bear.

"I think it's time for some reinforcements," Homer said, moving away from the pen.

"Such as?"

"Sticky cotton candy and an extra-large soda. Two straws."

Katherine didn't know about the two straw part, but she was thirsty. She strolled alongside Homer, who was walking on the painted pachyderm feet that showed the path to the elephant house, humming a tune from *Doctor Doolittle*. The man never seemed to run out of steam, never seemed to lack stimuli. In a way, she envied him. She was a person who planned her activities carefully, never going to a restaurant without having made reservations, never taking in a movie without reading at least two film reviews first. She liked being organized, but seeing an adult getting by without any specific planning, as Homer did, made her wonder if maybe she'd grown too rigid.

Even so, there was no way he could get her to eat cotton candy. "That stuff will kill your teeth," she said to him as he tore a huge hunk off his paper cone.

"And it sticks to you for days," he joyfully agreed.

They sat on a bench facing the elephants, who lumbered lazily around in a pool of muddy water.

"Wouldn't it be great to invent something really interesting?" Katherine asked. Immediately she knew she'd put her foot in her mouth. "Not that you haven't," she corrected.

Homer comically cocked one of his eyebrows over the mountain of pink he was holding. "What do you mean by 'really interesting'?"

"I mean, what if you invented something that revolutionized the way we live? Like the fax machine."

Homer grimaced. "I'd much rather go down in history as the inventor of the new and improved armadillo trap than the fax machine."

Katherine regarded him skeptically. "I don't believe you."

"It's true something like that would make an instant millionaire, and that would be nice. But I'd hate to think of all the lives I'd ruined."

"Ruined? But fax machines are amazing. Think of all the time they save people."

"Do they?" Homer asked. "I don't really see the fax machine that way. It just seems to make everything more urgent. Deadlines can be pushed to the limit now, and people have come to expect things to be done instantaneously. People in the cities even fax their restaurant orders, I hear, instead of walking down the street and actually talking to another human being face-to-face. Is that an improvement?"

Katherine took in his words and said nothing. He had a point; not all advances turned out to be as helpful as they first appeared. Still, progress was progress, and their contrasting perspectives on fax machines served to bring the overall differences between them into higher relief.

"We still haven't seen my favorite part of the zoo," she said.

"What's that?" Homer asked.

"The reptile house."

Homer smiled. "What, uh, exactly is it that you like to see there?"

"Snakes," she answered.

"Snakes?" Homer wrinkled his nose. "Back where I'm from, those are the last things anybody wants to see."

"I know," Katherine said. "That's why I like to see them. Behind glass. It makes me feel safe."

Fifteen minute later, Homer understood. Standing in front of a twenty-foot python, Katherine looked entirely at ease. The cold damp corridor wasn't exactly to his liking, but seeing Katherine happy, almost smugly so, was worth feeling a little closed in.

## Chapter Four

Homer had never met a woman as obsessed with her apartment as Katherine was. She always wanted to get back to it, and when they finally did return, it was difficult to get her to make plans to go out again. When she checked her answering machine and found no message from Bill Warren waiting for her, she reluctantly agreed to order takeout. But not before she had dragged out her much-talked-about tuna salad and tried to convince him they could have a perfectly nice dinner without even leaving the building.

But when she burped open the tuna salad's plastic tub, the meat was revealed to be a little on the old side. Katherine looked at Homer, defeat written all over her face.

"With the trip to Texas, I guess I forgot how long ago I whipped this stuff up."

Homer soberly took the tuna off her hands. "It is a little crusty. Like I said, we could just go out for pizza."

"Pizza?" Katherine asked nervously. But the pickings in her kitchen were slim, and maybe it would be better to go out. It would seem less intimate, even if she wouldn't be able to intercept Mr. Warren's phone call, which she was expecting at any moment. "I—I don't know any pizza places around here."

"None?" Homer asked incredulously.

"Well, I've seen them on the street of course, on my way to work. But I always eat at home whenever possible. I mean, I couldn't say which are good or bad, and I'm sure you would probably want pineapple topping or something strange like that."

Homer shook his head. Katherine was a case. "No pineapple. Just good old pepperoni."

"Oh, well . . ."

"And I saw a place this morning that's just around the corner."

Getting Katherine out her front door was another problem. She seemed to have difficulty deciding what to take on her journey to the pizza place. She debated the weight of jacket she should wear, whether she should feed her fish and whether to leave a new message on her machine to inform callers she would only be out for a short while.

"It's just for a few minutes," Homer said. She acted as if she doubted she'd ever see her place again.

She threw a final concerned glance over her shoulder as they locked up the apartment. Even safely zipped in to a medium-weight denim jacket, Katherine reminded Homer of a turtle that had just walked out of its shell. She huddled in the far corner of the elevator, as far from him as she could get in so small a space.

At that moment, more than anything else in the world, he wanted her to trust him. But dammit, everything he

did from there on out seemed to alienate her even more.
First, he embarrassed her by introducing her to one of
her own neighbors, a nice single mother he'd met that
morning on the elevator. Then he kindly asked a young
man on the street to please turn down his boom box,
since it was playing quite loudly. But the final blow was
when he saw a piece of carpet moving on the sidewalk.

"Did you hear something?" Homer asked, stopping
a few feet beyond it and looking back. "I think that pile
of carpeting was talking to us."

"Come on, Homer in Wonderland," Katherine said,
tugging at his arm.

Just then a head of hair the color of a Coke can
popped out from beneath the carpet. The face sur-
rounded by the incredible mane was pale and gaunt.
"Mister, you got a quarter?"

"It's a woman!" Homer exclaimed.

Katherine glanced from the poor woman to Homer
and felt a wave of dread at their apparent mutual fasci-
nation. Homer Ludlum meets the homeless, she
thought, fishing through her jacket pocket for change.

Homer walked back to the woman. "What's your
name?" he asked before Katherine could steer him away.

"Nadine Potter," the woman said. "I was burned out
of my apartment three months ago."

"And you've been living here?" Homer asked,
aghast. He had heard of the homeless problem, had even
run across a few bums and winos in his time, but he'd
never seen anything this desperate. He felt Katherine's
hand clamp his arm and turned to her. "Did you hear
that?" he asked.

"We need to get going," Katherine said, giving the
woman some change.

"This would never happen back home," Homer said.

"Where do you come from, mister?" the carpet lady asked. "Mars?"

"No, ma'am," Homer replied earnestly. "Texas."

The woman shivered a little in the chill of the evening, and Homer shrugged his jacket off his shoulders. "Here, take this," he said, handing it to the woman. Beside him, Katherine was muttering his name impatiently.

Nadine Potter refused the jacket. "Mister, you better listen to your lady friend there. You start giving your clothes to every person you see on the street and you'll be wearing your birthday suit by the end of the block."

Homer cursed under his breath and brought his wallet out of his back pocket. He pulled out a ten and offered it to the woman. "I'm afraid you need more than a quarter, Ms. Potter. Will you take this?"

"Listen, I appreciate what you're trying to do, Texas, but if word got out that I had that much money on me, I'd be in big trouble."

"Hide it," Homer said, thrusting the bill into her hands. "And if you need anything, my name's Homer. Katherine and I are just down the street, in the apartment building on the corner."

Katherine cringed as he gestured toward her building. Nadine Potter's unbelieving eyes followed his pointed finger.

"Texas, how long have you been in this town?" Nadine asked.

Homer was beginning to think he was the only rational person left in the nation's capital. "About twenty-four hours," he said. "And please, call me Homer."

The lady let out an unattractive snort. "That figures. Mister, I could as soon live in that apartment building as the Taj Mahal."

With that, Nadine Potter's amazing red head disappeared again under the carpet remnant.

Homer blinked, and Katherine took his arm and pulled him down the street. "Did you hear what that woman said?" he asked.

"You just can't do things like that, Homer," Katherine lectured. "That woman doesn't know you from Adam."

"I was trying to help."

"She probably thought you were mad as a hatter, and I'm beginning to think so, too."

"You mean she was suspicious of me?" His head was spinning in circles trying to make sense of the two women's logic.

"Wouldn't you be if you were on the streets? Strangers aren't always so kind."

Homer couldn't understand a place where everybody expected everyone else to turn on them and where even the destitute thought charity was an imposition.

Katherine felt a twinge of guilt. Explaining the facts of city life to Homer made her feel so callous. She gave money to people on the streets, but never much, and she would never have thought of telling anyone where she lived. And she was glad, even though her conscience was pricked at her relief, at getting Homer away before he had done any more damage. Knowing Homer, five minutes more and he'd have been giving the woman the keys to her apartment.

"The city is supposed to help the homeless," she clarified.

"Doesn't look like it's doing a very good job," Homer muttered.

It was true, and Katherine didn't know what to say. Living in such an inhumane place was embarrassing;

even worse to have to make excuses for it. Actually, she'd never been in that uncomfortable position before. Not until Homer.

Suddenly she felt annoyed. Annoyed that Homer Ludlum knew her neighbors better than she did, knew her neighborhood better than she did. In striving to become stable and self-sufficient, she had cut herself off from the very spirit of community she had missed as a child. In one day, Homer had discovered and revealed to her all the things she had shut herself off from.

Katherine's silence indicated that she agreed with him about the sorry state of affairs in the nation's capital, and Homer began to worry about her. Urban living could be as rugged as the Old West, and as ruthless apparently. The thought of stubborn Katherine living in the middle of all this madness nearly drove him wild. She needed a protector.

*He* needed sustenance, and pizza wouldn't do it. Seeing an Ethiopian restaurant, he stopped and suggested they duck inside. That was yet another mistake.

Katherine planted her feet firmly on the pavement in front of the restaurant's heavy wooden door. "Don't you ever do what you set out to do?" she huffed.

"Of course," Homer replied.

"Name one instance," she retorted, not giving an inch.

"I wanted to lure you out to dinner," Homer said honestly, opening the door for her.

He expected Katherine to march straight back to her apartment, but she went in ahead of him, picking a table far from the window. She read her menu with a determination that made him wince. Every movement seemed meant to communicate that she wasn't sitting across the table from him by choice. Her next statement confirmed this suspicion.

"I don't see how my company managed to dig up a Texan who isn't satisfied with plain old meat and potatoes," she grumbled.

"You're actually pretty lucky," Homer said. "I'm practically the only man in Ludlum who eats meat at all."

Katherine dropped her menu in disbelief. "Don't tell me I was in the only vegetarian town in Texas and didn't even realize it."

"It's true," Homer said. "In Ludlum, I'm considered something of a maverick."

To Homer's amazement, Katherine laughed out loud. "I hate to disillusion you, Homer," she said, "but I think people would consider you a maverick no matter where you went."

Her laughter broke the tension between them. After the waiter took their orders, they began to talk about their pasts, and Katherine related some humorous stories about her colorful mother. But Homer sensed there was some leftover unhappiness in that relationship that she was keeping from him.

For her part, Katherine was surprised to discover that Homer's early life had been as uneventful as hers was nomadic. He had grown up in Ludlum with his three brothers and sister, so far from the nearest neighbor that they only had themselves for playmates. She laughed at the stories of his school, which was so small that he was once promoted an extra year because he would have been the only pupil in the second grade.

After they had stuffed themselves on a variety of foods, all served on unleavened bread, they sat back and sipped their bittersweet coffee like old friends. For

Katherine, it was a feeling more exotic than the meal she'd just eaten.

"So why aren't Ludlumites carnivores?" she asked.

"That's because of my grandfather, Otis Ludlum. He was the son of the man they named the town after. Otis was a corn farmer, like my dad. But during the depression he got a little panicky and decided that the family needed something to fall back on in case there was a drought like the one in the dust bowl. So he bought a cow—he could only afford one. He used to joke that it was a 'cash cow,' and he treated that animal like a queen. He even named her Norma, after Norma Shearer, his favorite movie actress.

"Well, to make a long story short, there were a number of pretty lean years, but Norma just kept getting fatter and fatter. And Otis grew so attached to her that he sort of got a little woosy every time my grandmother scraped together enough money for a pot roast. Finally he forbade anybody in the family to eat any kind of meat—and the family's half the town. And most of them haven't, not since 1948, the year Otis died. His last words were, 'Don't eat Norma.'"

Katherine couldn't help chuckling at the tale any more than she could hold back a pang of envy—Homer's life seemed so full in comparison to hers. His history went deep and was alive with interesting characters like his grandfather. And when he spoke of his brothers and sister, it was with a fondness that matched no feeling in her own experience.

"I'd like to have grown up in your family," she said wistfully.

"It wasn't all fun and games," Homer said with a sigh. "Farming's risky and it gets tense sometimes—

waiting for rain or praying to heaven it won't flood. And it can be lonely, too, and sometimes downright dull."

"I can't imagine you being bored," Katherine protested.

"That's why I started the *Ludlum Free Press,*" Homer said. "I've always wanted to know about people, about what's happening around me. Of course, Ludlum is small and half our subscribers get the paper free, so inventions like the armadillo trap are what keep the paper going."

"I've been meaning to ask you about that," Katherine jumped in. "Why exactly did you go to all that trouble to put a reversible latch on something that's supposed to keep the armadillos in?"

Homer smiled. "So it won't catch the coons," he said.

Katherine was puzzled. "Raccoons? How can raccoons manage to get out?"

"Because the latch is shiny, it draws their attention. Raccoons can figure the trick out in no time. Armadillos aren't that bright."

Katherine remembered the scene in Warren's office, but didn't add that some humans weren't that bright, either. "But aren't raccoons pests, too?"

Homer's face reddened a shade. "Yeah," he agreed. "But they're a lot cuter than armadillos."

Katherine laughed. "Anything born of such a worthy cause deserves to make a lot of money," she said.

"I don't know if the coons had much to do with it, but I've gotten a lot of offers for that latch, all right."

That caught Katherine's attention. "How many offers?"

"Well, besides a summons from a certain toy company, about everybody from the federal government to a canning company has expressed interest. I've even had a toy company in New York City make me an offer.''

Katherine nodded, a smile plastered on her face in spite of the fact that her stomach was twisting in knots. Was there a chance Homer wasn't even interested in the Patriot contract? She hadn't considered that possibility. Would Warren blame her for not trying to bring him around? What if, when Homer had disappeared this morning, he'd gone to meet his government contact. She regarded him suspiciously as she mentally upbraided herself. *You've forgotten all about the invention because you've been so caught up with the inventor!*

"I'm sure a government contract would be very lucrative," she said, testing him.

Her tone wasn't lost on Homer. "I'm certainly interested in making money, Katherine. It would allow me to do what I've always wanted to do."

"What's that?" Katherine asked, curious.

"I want to start up a regular column in the paper," Homer said. "Maybe collect them into a book later."

"What kind of column?"

"Well," Homer began, obviously eager to discuss this topic, "I want to write a collection of people's stories. Narratives of people I've met and plan to meet when I do research for the paper. And with the money I make from the latch, I'll be able to do a lot more traveling."

Katherine practically had to clap her hand over her mouth to stifle a moan. How could she have forgotten? Here she was getting sentimental and charmed again, just because of some sweet stories and Homer's soft spot for animals, all the while forgetting that he embodied the trait she most detested. But she had underestimated Homer Ludlum. He wasn't just a vagabond, he was a calculating vagabond.

She could have kicked herself. Oh, she had been annoyed by his whimsical changes in plans, his gregariousness with the neighbors she barely knew by sight. Not so annoyed, though, that Homer couldn't break down her defenses with that smile of his, that sparkle in his eye when he said something amusing. Even so, she could forgive him for charming her, and herself for being charmed. But all the while to have been hatching plans to travel the country collecting stories from strangers was where Katherine drew the line. They were incompatible, and she should be horsewhipped for floundering in her resistance to Homer Ludlum.

The memory of their kiss that day had been lingering in the back of her mind all evening. But now she pushed it completely out of her consciousness. Homer Ludlum was enemy territory, and no amount of wishful thinking could change that.

"I hope you're very successful," she said, glancing pointedly at the check. All thought of wooing him for Patriot vanished. The man was dangerous. "I hope you get to write that book."

"I'm going to call it 'The Plight of the Common Man.'"

Katherine's stomach lurched as she thought of all the little adventures he was planning right there across the dimly lit table. "That sounds interesting," she lied. It sounded like a nightmare. Memories of her mother and her Passion Red nails came to mind, making her cringe. "I think we'd better get back," she said grimly.

Bill Warren had forsaken her again, Katherine discovered as she played through her messages when they arrived back at her apartment. Hovering over the flat black box, she listened to the words of storm-window salesmen, newspaper-subscription pedlars and a few hang-ups. She rarely received personal calls, which had never bothered her before. But having Homer standing nearby, listening to the host of impersonal messages, none of which was from her boss, was embarrassing.

"I'll get the blankets," Homer said when the tape had rewound itself.

Homer didn't quite know what had gone wrong in the restaurant. Apparently, his mentioning that Patriot had competition for his reversible latch bothered her a lot. It saddened him to think Katherine took her job so seriously. He had thought they were making progress during dinner, but judging by the way Katherine had scampered ahead of him all the way home, he supposed his assumption had been a bit premature.

Grabbing the pillow from the top of the pile of sheets he had used the night before, Homer let out a muttered oath. Katherine was jumpier now than she'd ever been. And he had vowed to put her at ease. Their relationship seemed doomed to be a roller-coaster ride, which doubtlessly would end the moment her company stopped courting him. Before his courtship of Katherine had even begun.

He thought about their kiss. He was certain her reaction had been genuine, that the abandon she'd shown briefly hadn't stemmed only from lust or loneliness. And her pulling away so abruptly had all the earmarks of the self-denial she practiced in all aspects of her life, from her functional furniture to the distance she seemed to put between herself and everything around her. She might harbor some sentiment for his tight-knit family and his rural home, but she sure didn't know how to make those simple dreams a reality for herself.

When he arrived in the living room with the bed things, Katherine was feeding her fish. She lavished a lot of attention on those creatures, he thought with a pang of jealousy.

"Maybe you should name one of those things Norma," he commented, unable to keep the caustic tone from his voice.

"I don't give them names," she said.

Homer was taken aback. "Why not?" he asked.

Katherine shrugged. "They're cute, but there's no sense in becoming too attached to them. Fish can be alive and kicking one minute and belly-up the next. I'd hate to name one and then have to flush it down the toilet."

Her sad, practical words tore at Homer. He knew it was the wrong thing to do, but he did it, anyway. He grabbed Katherine's arm and tugged her onto the couch with him. She landed on his lap, but she didn't appear too happy about it. She perched on his knee like a swallow on a live wire.

"Is something wrong, Katherine?"

"Oh, no," she said. "You maneuvered that quite well." She clasped her hands together in her lap and held her body stiff as a board.

"I meant, what happened at the restaurant, Katherine?"

She made a point of avoiding eye contact, but other than that, nothing in Katherine's demeanor suggested there was anything intimate about their situation. Which was more than he could say for his own body's fevered reaction. He shiftly slightly to ease the tightening in his gut, inadvertently jarring Katherine to answer.

"Nothing," she blurted.

"Then why are you acting as though I've made you angry?"

He felt a tremor run through her body and grasped her more tightly. But instead of bursting into tears or a rage, both of which he was prepared for, she merely turned toward him, her face deadpan. "There's no reason for anything you say to make me angry, Homer. Would you like to know why?"

Not really, he thought, but he went along with her anyway. "Why?"

"Because we're like apples and oranges. We have so little in common that there's no basis for any kind of emotional connection to develop between us." She picked herself up out of his lap and sat down primly on the other end of the couch.

Homer might not have been able to make Katherine angry, but her prissy little speech had riled him up but good. He shifted closer to her, enjoying the discomfort that flashed across her eyes.

"What do you think is so different about us, Katherine?"

A little spasm zipped through her. She didn't like the mocking tone in his husky voice or the puckish glint in his eyes. This wasn't going as planned. "Well," she began, unable to keep a tremor out of her voice, "there are some people who think the world is their oyster."

"I suppose that's me," Homer said, leaning a little closer. He reached over to touch her hair and she ducked.

"Uh-uh, and there are some people—"

"Like you?"

"Yes." She swatted his hand away when he reached for her hair again.

"And what do those people think?"

Katherine hesitated. He was getting her muddled. "Never mind what I think! The point is, people like you think everybody else should drop whatever they're doing at your slightest whim."

"Really?"

"Yes."

Even though she didn't dare look at him, she could feel Homer smiling at her. "And I suppose people like you expect everyone else to plod along at the same steady pace, never straying an inch from the set path," he said.

With a frustrated sigh, Katherine turned on him. "You know that's not true."

"Why not?"

"You're deliberately making my way of thinking sound as dull as dirt."

"It is, the way you describe it."

"I didn't..." she sputtered angrily. "That's just the trouble between us, Homer. We may be the same species, but we don't speak the same language."

"Oh, we don't?" he drawled, edging closer.

"No."

Homer smiled and stretched an arm across the back of the couch, which coincidentally landed right across Katherine's shoulder. She huddled a little closer to the armrest, whereupon he placed a firm hand on her knee. When finally they were sitting about as close as two people could get, short of climbing on top of each other—which Homer would have dearly loved—he nuzzled her ear.

"You know," he said lazily, "it's a funny thing about species."

Katherine froze. His breath caressing her ear was agonizingly pleasurable. "What's that?" she asked.

"They usually come in pairs. So even if they don't speak the same language, they can always find a way to communicate."

Katherine let out a little yelp, but before she could escape, she was engulfed in the warmest, sweetest kiss she'd ever experienced. And before she could think better of it, she turned toward the perpetrator of that kiss and wrapped her arms around his neck. Which was the wrong thing to do.

Homer's body pressed hard against hers, which seemed to arch against him of its own volition. His hands massaged her temple, her neck, and moved languidly up and down her back. Those hands seemed to be doing the most damage to Katherine's self-control, pushing her closer to him, making her body clamor to have the thin barrier of her T-shirt gone.

His lips traced the hollow of her throat, bringing an exquisite ache all over her. She had a vague awareness of having shifted slightly, and she noted briefly that she now lying across the couch. Homer reached a hand down to massage one of her breasts, making her breathe in short rapid gusts. When his hand moved under her shirt, she had to bite her lip to stifle a small cry.

It came out seconds later, anyway, when a loud buzz sounded through the room. Both of them bolted upright and sprang apart like two teenagers caught necking at a church social.

"What was that?" Katherine exclaimed.

"I believe it was your doorbell." Doorbuzz, was more like it, Homer thought. It was damned annoying.

"What should I do?"

"Answer it, I guess."

"Of course." Katherine composed herself, smoothing her hair back and standing on jittery legs. What had happened to her? She was completely losing her grip—and she'd come back to the apartment with such good intentions! Although one tiny part of her felt as giddy as a schoolgirl, the nobler sector of her brain squelched that feeling fast. What had occurred on that couch was the second blunder she had made that day, and she wasn't going to allow herself to get carried away again.

She marched to the door with renewed determination. She should thank the person on the other side of that door. And she planned to, except that when she opened it, Mrs. Hobbs brushed right past her.

"Homer Ludlum!" Gladys bustled excitedly toward Homer. "I want to shake your hand!"

Homer's expression turned from perplexed to panicked as Mrs. Hobbs not only shook his hand, but engulfed his entire body in an enormous hug. Then she turned a positively beatific smile on Katherine.

"What has he done now?" Katherine asked.

Homer shrugged innocently over Mrs. Hobbs's silvery head.

"Why, he's just the kindest, most thoughtful man I've ever met! Would you believe, Katherine, I was walking Millie this evening, just down the street like I always do, and Millie stopped to do her business by this mound of shag carpet—"

Katherine's and Homer's horror-stricken faces met simultaneously. "Oh, no!" Katherine cried.

"Well," Mrs. Hobbs continued, oblivious to their reaction, "I've never been so embarrassed in my life. There was a person under that carpet!"

"Nadine Potter?" Homer asked, knowing the answer.

"Yes! Well, Millie about jumped out of her fur when she saw that carpet come to life. The woman was hopping mad, but what could I do? I explained to her that sleeping under a rug was just asking for it, with so many dogs in the neighborhood like there are, and so few trees. And then, the woman flashed a ten-dollar bill in my face and announced that she didn't have to live in this neighborhood anymore and that she was moving herself elsewhere. Can you imagine?

"So I asked her, 'Honey, where on earth did you find so much money?' And she said, 'Homer Texas gave it to me.' And I said, 'You must mean Homer *Ludlum,*' and I described you for her, and she agreed you were who she meant."

"So what happened?" Katherine asked.

"Well," Mrs. Hobbs answered as if it should be perfectly obvious, "Nadine's up in my apartment right now taking a bath."

"What?" Katherine and Homer cried at once.

Mrs. Hobbs looked at both of them in turn. "After Millie piddled on the poor thing, it was the least I could do. And she is one of Homer's friends." The old lady turned to Katherine. "You won't believe this, but that woman whipped up some chocolate-chip cookies that are the best thing this side of heaven."

To Katherine's surprise, it was Homer who spoke next. "Gladys, you can't just keep that woman in your apartment. You don't know anything about her."

Mrs. Hobbs was taken aback. "Of course I do! She told me all about herself while she was baking the cookies."

"Homer means that you don't know where she comes from, what kind of person she is."

"Oh, yes, I do," Gladys insisted. "Nadine lived right in this neighborhood before her apartment building burned down. Imagine, Katherine, right down the street from us! And before that, she lived with her no-account husband who chased everything in a skirt and then ran off. Why, her story about had me in tears, so I told her how I was a widow and about dear Frank. And do you know what she said? She said, 'Gladys, you were a lucky woman to find Frank Hobbs.'"

Gladys collapsed on the couch with a sob. "That about broke my heart. I know she's a good person. I just know it."

Homer sat down next to Gladys and patted her shoulder, looking helplessly at Katherine.

"Oh, Katherine," the elderly woman cried, "I just hope you and Homer find as much as happiness together as Frank and I did."

"I'll get some tea," Katherine said, fleeing into the kitchen. Here she was going to thank Mrs. Hobbs for keeping her from the biggest mistake in her life, and then she discovered that Gladys had probably already made the mistake of *her* life—taking in a homeless woman!— all because of Homer. The man had thrown all their lives into an uproar. And not only that, but Gladys practically had her married off to him.

Katherine quickly put the tea things together and headed back to the living room, where Mrs. Hobbs was talking Homer's ear off. But when Gladys saw the tea tray, she protested, "Just a splash for me, Katherine. I've got to get back to Nadine. I surely didn't mean to interrupt anything."

Homer shot Katherine a glance that indicated he hadn't forgotten one moment of what Gladys had interrupted. His brilliant blue eyes promised that he'd pick up right where they had left off, but Katherine wasn't about to let that happen. She took a fortifying slug of Earl

Grey tea and steeled her nerves against Homer's intense gaze.

Homer had barely heard a word Mrs. Hobbs was saying. She was talking about the nation's homeless, he knew, but all he could think about was what was going on in Katherine's mind. This latest turn of events probably hadn't helped his case any. Not one bit, if he could judge by the way Katherine was swilling her tea.

"Well, I've got to run," Mrs. Hobbs said finally. "You two have fun!"

But when she left, the room was about as lively as a bank loan office. Katherine stood across the room from Homer, the air between them tense and charged. He started to close the distance between them, but stopped when Katherine recoiled like a grass snake in front of a steamroller.

"What's the matter?" he asked softly.

Katherine squared her shoulders. "Not a thing."

"Well, then—"

"Not a thing, that is," she corrected, "except that my whole life is out of whack—and so, apparently, is my neighbor's."

Homer stepped forward and took her stiff body into his arms. "You're beautiful when you're off-balance."

Katherine ducked out of his embrace. "I'm not beautiful," she said, pushing away from him. "I'm just trying to do my job, which is to deliver you to my boss at nine o'clock on Monday morning."

Homer let loose his laziest Texas smile and asked, "And after that?"

"After that," Katherine said coolly, "I'm going to continue with my life. Except now I've got all sorts of neighbors and a vagrant to deal with."

Homer looked at her seriously. "I intend to make sure you have more than just neighbors to deal with."

"What does that mean?"

"I'm not going to exit your life just because you've done your duty to the company, Katherine."

"Homer, please," she pleaded. "We have very little in common. I think we should leave it at that."

"I don't think you really believe the situation is as hopeless as you make it sound."

"After two days, you're hardly in a position to know what I really believe," she argued vehemently.

"Maybe not, but about half an hour ago I was in a perfect position to know how you felt about one aspect of our relationship." Homer looked pointedly at the couch and then at her as a deep red flush crept up her cheeks. "And I'm not about to let it end there."

Katherine's mouth dropped open and snapped shut in the course of a split second. Not knowing any appropriate response, she turned on her heel and fled to her room.

# Chapter Five

"Where's Homer Ludlum?"

With rigid control, Katherine put *Brenda Starr* aside and followed her boss down the hall. He usually shut himself in his office in the morning, but she knew this was going to be an exception. It was nine o'clock Monday morning, and she hadn't seen Homer since eleven-thirty the night before.

"So where is he, Henry?" Warren snapped again when they sat peering at each other over the paper jungle that was his desk.

"I have no idea," Katherine said evenly.

"What!" Warren's voice rose and his face fell.

"I know what you're going to say, Mr. Warren," Katherine began, her voice shaky but determined. She had been working on gathering her composure since six-thirty that morning, when she'd found the note Homer had left on the refrigerator.

"What have you done with him, Henry?"

"That's what I thought you were going to say," she conceded. "But you can rest assured I haven't done anything with him. I didn't have to. The man is a walking lost-and-found."

"Jiminy Cricket!" Warren's eyes rolled heavenward. "You lost him! Do you have any idea what the Boys have planned for Homer Ludlum today?"

Katherine cringed. She was undoubtedly about to find out.

"A tour of our Virginia manufacturing plant," he began, "a meeting with five of our top designers and a five-course luncheon with one of our wealthiest shareholders and the president of the company. Mr. Wittington himself."

Warren made it sound as if Homer were slated to meet the president of the United States, instead of the president of a toy company. "Is that all?" she asked.

Warren gaped at her in astonishment. "All?" he asked, the word barely audible.

"Because there's something you should know, Mr. Warren," Katherine declared, "and you can tell this to the Boys. Keeping up with Homer Ludlum is a ten-man assignment at least, Mr. Warren, and I'm not being facetious. Have you ever been to the Gross National Parade?"

Warren shook his head, perplexed. "No. No, I haven't."

"I have," Katherine fumed. "That's where I found Homer on Saturday. Right next to the Virginia Beekeeper's Association. Unfortunately, while I was looking for him he befriended half the people in my building. That was before he hooked up with a homeless woman named Nadine, who now, by the way, lives with my upstairs neighbor."

She skipped the other things that happened on Saturday, not wanting to dredge up memories that were best left forgotten.

"Yesterday I woke up and discovered that Homer had taken a group of senior citizens from my building to visit the National Cathedral, where I finally chased them down at Woodrow Wilson's tomb. Everyone was having such a good time that Homer decided we should all go to Mount Vernon. He staged a stone-throwing contest to see if it was really possible to hurl a rock across the Potomac. That's when Mr. Scarlatti from the second floor dislocated his shoulder. You might think that Homer Ludlum had really worn out those old people, right?"

Warren raised an eyebrow doubtfully.

"But no," Katherine continued. "After we got Mr. Scarlatti out of the emergency room, everyone decided that we had to go for Cajun food and dancing, where I was shoved up on stage next to an accordion player and handed a washboard. Mr. Warren, Homer Ludlum is such a rootless maniac that he had to invent a suitcase that could keep up with him. And if I have to listen to one more song from the mellow seventies' hit parade, I honestly think I'm just going to spiritually crumble."

Warren scurried out to the water dispenser in the hallway and brought back a paper cup of water for his frazzled assistant. As she gulped it down, he patted her heartily on the back.

"Above and beyond, Henry," he grumbled proudly.

"What?" Katherine asked, squishing the paper cup into a soggy little ball.

"You've served your post above and beyond the call of duty, Henry. Don't think I'll forget this."

Don't think I will, either, Katherine thought.

"So where is he now?" Warren asked.

Katherine shrugged. "He left a note on the refrigerator door this morning. 'Errands,' it read. Now, from what I've just described, what do *you* think 'errands' means to Homer Ludlum?"

Warren looked through a chink in the venetian blinds. "Above and beyond," he murmured again.

*Above and beyond.* Katherine repeated the words to herself. Warren didn't know the half of it. He thought of her as the perfect company man, but what would he have said if she had told him that his precious cargo had practically seduced her on her very own couch?

Katherine let out a long breathy sigh. In truth, she'd had second thoughts as she lay in bed on Sunday morning. The Ethiopian food had been good, and she couldn't remember laughing as much as she had in the two days she'd spent with Homer. And Homer had very thoughtfully slid the comics underneath her door before he left.

But he *had* left, she reminded herself, and that's what he would spend his whole life doing. Leaving. Heading out for parts unknown with a trail of refrigerator notes and cryptic messages in his wake. Getting involved with Homer would mean chasing him down, putting up with a host of strangers who would drift into her life only to leave again, and seeing a lot of places—and never being able to settle down in one of them and roost.

At least she wasn't fool enough to think she could change him, she thought with equal parts pride and misery. She had spent an entire childhood hoping her mother would make concessions for her sake, which Marge had never done, and she wasn't going to make that mistake again. Because if there was one thing Katherine had learned from her mother, it was that some people were simply restless, and they exercised their wanderlust with a fury no one else could control.

A shadow darkened Bill Warren's doorway, and Katherine's head shot up expectantly. She expelled a rush of air and felt relieved beyond belief. Homer had made it. She almost smiled at him, before remembering his defection that morning.

Their eyes locked. His were soft, concern showing clearly in them. Katherine darted a piercing glare at him and willed her own eyes to send him a message: *You're a mobile demon, Homer Ludlum.*

Homer got the message, and he felt about two inches tall. Dammit, he'd made her mad again. And from the way she was crouching in that chair, it looked like he hadn't helped her any with her boss, either. Good grief, he couldn't seem to stop digging himself in deeper and deeper. He hoped she would approve of the way he'd spent the early part of the morning.

"Mr. Ludlum!" Bill Warren exclaimed when he spotted Homer looming in his doorway.

Katherine smirked. Without introduction, Warren had guessed who the stranger was. Homer had the muscled lankiness of a Texan and the unmistakable thoughtful look of a man who dreamed for a living. Just seeing him now, meeting the knowing look in his incredible blue eyes, turned her insides to jelly.

*He's just like any of the dozens of memos you type up each day,* she reminded herself. And he was now about to be tossed into her out-tray.

"Sit down, sit down," Warren said, motioning Homer to a large leather chair beside the one Katherine was sitting in. "I'm glad you could make it this morning."

Homer sat, his long limbs jutting out of the chair like a daddy longlegs. He shot Katherine an unsure glance.

"I'm sorry to be a little late," he replied genially to Warren. "I had some business to take care of."

"Of course," Warren agreed, beaming.

Katherine shifted uneasily, not sure whether she was required to stay now that her duty had been performed. To tell the truth, she felt a little nervous about leaving Homer alone in Warren's office, like a mother dropping a child off for his first day of school.

"Henry here tells me you've had quite a weekend," Warren continued. "You like Washington, Mr. Ludlum?"

"Sure," Homer said. "I like the people." The statement was not lost on Katherine, nor, she could tell, was it meant to be. But it hardly warranted the bouncy, hopeful little lift she felt deep inside her.

"I especially like the accommodations," Homer said more pointedly.

Warren winked at Katherine, who felt like sinking through the floor. Then her employer jumped right into business, giving Homer a briefing on the day's planned events. A master of salesmanship, Bill Warren blew every meeting just the right amount out of proportion to make Homer Ludlum feel like the most important man in the world. According to Warren, the big men in the carpeted offices of Patriot Games and Toys were awaiting Homer's arrival as they would a visit from a minor potentate.

She caught a glimpse of Homer, though, and knew immediately that he wasn't taken in by the pitch. Every muscle of his body bespoke boredom. He shifted often and gave his jaw muscle a mini-workout. He examined the knuckles of his left hand with the intensity of an elderly couple sitting on a porch swing watching the grass grow. But all the while, he paid just enough attention to Warren to keep up a semblance of interest.

Finally Mr. Warren said he needed to make a phone call before they got started. As he angled away from them, Katherine took the opportunity to speak to Homer in a low whisper.

"Where were you this morning?" she asked.

"Did you miss me?" Homer said with a wry grin.

"No, but my boss did. Didn't I tell you I was responsible for you?"

Homer's eyes sparkled. "If I'd known I was in your hands, I would have tried to take more advantage."

"You've taken plenty, thanks," Katherine murmured.

Homer reached over and captured her hand. "I'm sorry, Katherine. I know you think I'm irresponsible, but you're wrong. I had to take Nadine to her job."

"What?" She lowered her voice when Warren glowered at her from the phone. "Nadine has a job?"

"It's not the greatest job. I think she could do better...." His voice trailed off thoughtfully.

Katherine was astounded. How had he found Nadine a job so quickly? Obviously, once Homer Ludlum set his mind on something, he didn't let go easily. The kindness he showed Nadine made her realize something. He was one of the kindest men she'd ever known. He was always on the go, but his actions were never without purpose. And he had eyes that she could look into forever, just as she was doing now....

They both looked up when they realized Bill Warren was off the phone. He picked at a speck of lint on his shirt and shrugged his shoulders uncomfortably, like a man who had inadvertently walked into a love nest. Katherine felt the blood rush to her face. That was the last thing she wanted her boss to think! When Warren finally looked up, she gave him her best deadpan, company-man gaze.

"Are you, uh, finished?" he asked a little too politely.

"Just a little roommate business," Homer quipped, smiling. Katherine winced when Warren winked at her again, looking amused.

"Well," he said, bounding out of his chair, "guess it's time for Homer and me to shove off." He hustled them both out of their chairs and toward the door.

As she watched Warren whisk Homer down the hall between their drab messy offices, she again felt uneasy about letting Homer out of her sight. She followed them, and when Homer flashed her a brief grin before he turned the corner and disappeared from sight, his finger touching his temple in mock salute, Katherine felt what could only be described as acute separation anxiety.

The rest of the morning dragged by. Katherine had been so worried about Homer after she'd gotten up that she had done something unthinkable: she'd forgotten to make herself a lunch. She held out for as long as she could, but nervousness about Homer only aggravated her hunger. By one o'clock her stomach was making angry noises and she decided to go out and grab a bite.

Leaving her building, though, she saw something that made her do a double take. A bright green van with the words "Tasty Morsel" written in pink script across the side was parked at the curb. At first she thought she must be so hungry she was imagining psychedelic catering vans. Then she saw the driver's red hair, hair a person only had to see once to remember, and knew immediately that this vision was no mirage—it was Nadine.

Nadine spotted her and honked up a storm. "Hey, girl!" she bellowed. "Come on over here!"

Gray-suited passersby stopped and stared at the spectacle of Nadine hanging out the van window, waving frantically, beckoning Katherine to join her. Then Katherine saw Homer waving from the passenger seat.

*Homer?*

She sprinted across the street as fast as her medium heels would allow, and Nadine hopped out of the driver's-side door to let her in. The three of them in the front seat made a tight squeeze. And Homer wasn't budging to make room for her, Katherine noticed. She was practically on his lap once Nadine had buckled up and pulled out into the traffic.

"What are you doing here?" she barked, conscious of sounding suspiciously like her boss.

"I took a break," Homer said, his eyes shining into hers like a spring day.

"But...but..." she protested.

Homer draped an arm around her shoulders and pulled her close. She didn't like that at all. "Don't worry," he said. "I'll be back by the time coffee is served. Those five-course luncheons go on forever."

She liked that even less.

"Where did this van come from?" Katherine asked.

"It's my new job!" Nadine exclaimed.

Katherine looked at Nadine and noticed her outfit— green pin-striped coveralls with the Tasty Morsel logo on a little patch on her chest. She now wore a Tasty Morsel sun visor to match.

"Pretty snazzy, huh? Honey, I am a deluxe high-class caterer. Or at least, I get to deliver food for deluxe, high-class people to eat."

Katherine turned and looked in the back of the van. Steel racks lined the sides and one section held several rows of covered platters.

"Are you making deliveries now?"

"I sure am, hon."

Katherine panicked, afraid of being gone from work too long. And they had to get Homer back to the Dupont Circle headquarters, which was retreating farther and farther into the distance. "Homer, how on earth did you find Nadine in the middle of a luncheon?"

"Simple," he said. "I called in an order." He was dying to be alone with Katherine. He couldn't stop thinking about her all morning, especially the way she had looked at him in Warren's office while her boss was on the phone. As if she was going to melt. Now she looked as if she was going to snap.

Nadine was quick to calm Katherine's fears. "Don't worry—it's some senator's birthday in half an hour, so I have to drive back your way soon, and I'll drop you both off."

Katherine relaxed a little upon hearing the woman's plan. "I'm starving," she admitted.

Homer reached down to the floorboard. "Try one of these," he said, taking a chocolate éclair from a foil-wrapped plate.

"I can't eat Tasty Morsel's food," Katherine protested.

"Nadine made these. They're delicious," Homer explained.

Katherine stared at the éclair with yearning and a little awe. "How did you learn to make these?"

"Honey, I didn't always live on the street." Nadine let out a merry hoot, as if the thought were just plain ridiculous. "And living on the street was an adventure after twelve years with Ned Potter—that's no lie. Ned was my husband," she added, flipping on her turn signal. "I was what I call a real housewife, meaning that when I married Ned Potter and thought I'd hit the big time, I really just married a house. Ned was a cheating, two-timing no-account—and you can print that in that book of yours, Mr. Ludlum."

Katherine turned to Homer for an explanation.

"Nadine's going to be the first story in 'The Plight of the Common Man,'" he said.

"Anyway," Nadine continued with a shrug, "I thought I could lure my husband home with food. A way to a man's heart and all that. Well, I spent about twelve years watching those cooking shows on PBS—you know, the ones they play in the afternoons. It didn't save my marriage but, baby, can I cook!"

She cackled lustily, and Katherine couldn't help but join her. Nadine's energy was infectious, Katherine decided, noticing that Homer, too, was smiling. Nadine parked the van and jumped out in front of a gracious colonial mansion.

"This won't take a second, kids," she said with a wink as she unloaded a few platters.

Katherine had been winked at three times in one day, and it only served to make being alone with Homer on the front seat all the more uncomfortable. Katherine edged a little closer to the steering wheel, away from his distracting thigh. "I'm a bit worried," she said tentatively, "but this was a nice surprise."

A grin tickled Homer's lips. "I thought you were the woman who didn't like surprises."

"I never said that," Katherine defended.

"Maybe it just depends on the kind of surprise," Homer suggested.

She didn't like the tone of his voice. Husky, probing. After so much Nadine, his low sexy drawl was disconcerting. Her rear end continued its slow creep toward the driver's seat. "Well—" Katherine began, then stopped.

Homer's hand clasped hers with a firm grip. "I think we need to talk," he said. "I suspect you're not telling me everything that's on your mind."

"Homer," she pleaded, "I don't think we can discuss anything right now. Not here."

"We can't pretend there's nothing between us."

"We—we're not," she stammered. "I mean, there isn't anything."

"Isn't there?" he asked, his thumb probing her palm meaningfully. It was hard to lie while that thumb sent electric shocks of desire racing up her arm. She didn't say anything, hoping she could silently will him away from the topic.

Homer knew for sure there was something between them. It was written all over Katherine's face that she cared about him, at least a little. A lot more than a little, he hoped. But women were the oddest creatures. And Katherine, while she tried so hard to lead a "normal" existence, was the oddest of all. He released her hand and leaned against the passenger door, observing her.

Katherine looked as if she was about to crumble. She sat rigidly straight on the seat, not daring to move a muscle. He couldn't figure her out. In his mind, things were simple. And if they weren't as simple as you wanted them to be, you simply puzzled them out until they became clear. That was what he was trying to do. Puzzle Katherine out.

Katherine nervously pushed back a stray wisp of hair, wishing with all her might that Nadine would rescue her. She had to get back to work. And she had to make sure Homer got back. Lord, her boss would think she was a traitor if he knew what she was doing on this particular lunch hour. Knowing Warren's temper, he'd fire her on the spot. And she wouldn't blame him for it, either, not one bit. Good company men didn't allow themselves to be kidnapped at lunchtime.

She was going to develop an ulcer right then and there, she decided, feeling a little queasy. Then her stomach let out a humiliating roar. She jumped at the noise.

Homer grabbed the éclair sitting on the dash. "Take a bite," he commanded.

"I'm okay," Katherine lied.

"That's not what your body's saying." He scooted toward her with the pastry.

Her body was saying all sorts of things she shouldn't listen to, Katherine thought dryly, getting as close to the driver's-side door as she could without spilling onto the pavement.

"C'mon, Kath," Homer cajoled, "you've got to eat."

She turned huffily toward him, and her nose practically collided with the sticky chocolate icing of the éclair. Then she met his eyes, saw his strong mouth, smelled his after-shave mixed with the sweetness of the sugary confection. "Homer—"

There was no telling what happened to that éclair. Homer's lips were on hers, exploring. The taste was twice as delectable as any food could have been, and she relished it. Her stomach rumbled, but not for food. With a growl, Homer pulled her across his lap and continued his sensual assault. Her body went limp in his arms.

Katherine had never known that a kiss could feel like this. She had never known that a man could make her forget her best intentions, her common sense. But as his large hands massaged her back with aching force, she forgot all the reasons she had for not letting things go this far. Her only question was: why had she been shying away from something this wonderful?

"You folks are gonna be bad for my business."

Nadine's words cut like a knife through the heat gathering in the van. "I hate to break this up..."

Katherine lurched out of Homer's arms with a vigor she hadn't thought herself capable of. She was trembling and flushed and so embarrassed she wished she could evaporate. And she was furious with herself. Reason, which had escaped her just moments before, came flooding back.

Nadine chattered away about the fancy house and the stuffed shirts who lived in it, but all Katherine could concentrate on was how to keep from jostling against Homer every time the van hit a bump or turned a corner. She couldn't wait to escape the confines of that vehicle! And when they pulled up in front of her office building, Katherine ignored Homer's hand, which touched her cheek lightly, and practically jet-propelled herself over Nadine and out the door.

She was so frantic that she forgot to look to make sure Homer followed her into the building and made it back to the luncheon.

Homer's balloons arrived an hour later. The card, neatly typed, read: "Roses are red, violets are blue, but helium balloons seemed more appropriate for you. H." They were the plastic silver kind she had seen in florist-shop windows. Most had flowers painted on them. One, though, had a sad-faced clown and "Get Well Soon" written across it in large block letters. The florist had flubbed, but the mistake made her laugh. She hoped some poor sick child in a hospital hadn't gotten a pink balloon with "I Love You, Darling" written in florid romantic script.

Then she cringed. What an imagination! Homer Ludlum hadn't spoken a word about love. Nor would he, if she had any say in the matter. As good as it felt to be in his arms, she would have no future with a man who courted women in a pastry truck.

She eyed the balloons suspiciously. They reeked of Homer Ludlum, all right. Flighty and practical. Romantic, too, in an odd way. Almost right, but not quite. And therein lay the problem.

She was lovesick, that was certain. But every time she looked at the signature, she couldn't help but wish the *H* stood for any other person except Homer. For the next hour she doodled on a yellow legal pad. Howard. Henry. Hank. Hector. All of those names sounded better than Homer, because she could imagine they represented a nice stable banker who dreamed of living in the suburbs or anybody besides a crazy Texas inventor whose greatest dream was "The Plight of the Common Man."

Those balloons took up too much space, she decided, pushing them over to the edge of her desk. But they seemed to have a will of their own, coming back no matter which way she shoved them. Finally she hooked them to the outside of her door. But they were still there, taunting her. Her generous office felt like a cage.

Katherine began to pace like a cheetah in the zoo. He cared for her, she knew. But how much? Had he sent the balloons because the meeting with the five top design-

ers bored him? Or was he serious about her? She didn't
know anymore which option she preferred. And she
wondered if she was making a big deal out of nothing.

"Trouble with you is you're uptight," her mother had
told her a thousand times. "You just can't take things as
they come."

But Marge Henry was wrong, Katherine knew. She
could take things as they came, within normal limits, just
the same as anybody else. But her mother had expected
her to accept switching schools every year—at least—as
normal. And not having any friends, because there just
wasn't time enough to make them. And most of all,
she'd had to learn to accept her mother herself, to make
excuses for a woman who couldn't hold a job, a man, a
home.

She thought of all the cheap motels she had lived in,
all the times she'd had to sleep on the Chevy's back seat,
because Marge would insist on driving all night until they
reached Memphis, or Billings, or wherever the next stop
was. She and Nadine had more in common than Homer
probably knew.

Katherine fumed for a good ten minutes. Then she
remembered that she hadn't really told Homer about her
childhood at all. She had lied about it by making light of
her wacky, flighty mother, just as she'd always done. She
hadn't mentioned the pain she felt at never having had
a home to call her own, to invite kids her own age to. She
joked about all these things, tried to cast humor on
them, because she couldn't face the fact that her mother
hadn't really been a real mother, just a loveless road
mom—just Marge, her vagabond parent.

Homer didn't know any of this. But because her feelings for Homer were much more than they should have
been, she expected him to know it intuitively. She was a

fool. Homer might not be the right man for her, but he
deserved better than the cold shoulder she'd given him
ever since the incident on the couch on Saturday night.
Just remembering his hands roaming lazily along her
back brought a shudder.

She was still hungry, and an idea hit her. A dinner
party! She would have a big dinner party, with Homer,
Mrs. Hobbs, Nadine and herself. It would be festive—
and there would be lots of people around so Homer
wouldn't think she was doing it for him, which she was,
and she knew it, but she didn't want him to get the
wrong idea. And then, after dinner, she would sit him
down and tell him her feelings, explaining that she found
him attractive but wasn't interested in having a relationship right now. It would be a very tidy end to their deal-
ings with each other.

Warren huffed by her doorway about an hour later.
"You sick?" He said it as though she damned well deserved to be.

"What?"

He nodded at the sad clown balloon but didn't wait
for an answer.

Out of habit, she grabbed her yellow legal pad, tear-
ing off the page with her party plans on it, and traipsed
down the hall behind her boss.

"Jiminy Cricket!" Warren growled, collapsing into
his chair. "The man's a lunatic. He's not only got a few
screws loose, he's got a whole head of hardware rattling
around!"

"It didn't go well?" Katherine asked sympathetically. She knew the answer, and she didn't know if she
had the heart to listen.

"Go well!" Warren snapped. "You were right about that man, Katherine. And don't think I won't remember that. Above and beyond, Henry," he ranted.

"What exactly happened?"

"Happened? What didn't happen, you mean. First, the man sings in the elevator all the way up to the twenty-first floor, which should have given me a clue right there. But I sing sometimes, too—in private, mind you. So I introduce him to Mr. Wittington like he's just another person, not a nut case. You know what he does?"

Katherine shook her head.

"He pulls these newspaper clippings out of his pocket. I mean, he's barely met the president of the company, and he's harassing him about corporations that don't pay their fair share of America's taxes and pollute the environment—on and on. Then we have the luncheon. Ludlum kept jumping up every ten minutes saying he had to use the phone. Then, when he finally does sit down, he takes one look at the filet mignon and starts telling us about his grandpa Otis and some damned cow. The man ruined Mr. Wittington's appetite."

Thinking of Norma, Katherine's lips twitched. She bobbed her head, though, encouraging her boss to continue.

"Then, right as we're settling down to business, the man pops out of his chair and disappears for an hour. An hour!"

Katherine flushed scarlet. This was the part that was going to cost her her job. She held her breath.

"You *are* sick, aren't you?"

"What?"

"You're all red and splotchy. You need some water?"

"No sir, I'm just fine. Did, uh, Homer get back okay?"

"Oh, sure. Got back right as they were serving coffee. Then he gets up and makes another phone call. I hope he's not running up your bill at home, Henry. Be sure you fill out an expense report."

Katherine hoped that was the end of the interview. She shot out of her seat as if it was, feeling like a traitor to her company.

"You can rest easy, though, Henry. We finally got Homer Ludlum out of your hair."

Katherine froze. "What?" she asked. "How?"

"Well, whattaya expect? I took one look at that nut case and thought, 'Warren, you gotta get this guy a hotel room.'"

Katherine felt as though she might burst into tears. That was it, then. Suddenly she wanted to tell Bill Warren that she had never slept so well until she'd met Homer Ludlum. And that she had laughed and that she'd actually been planning her first dinner party.

Warren let out a big bear of a yawn and propped his feet on the desk. Clasping his hands at the back of his neck, he scrutinized his assistant, who was now slumped against the doorjamb. "You really do look sick," he said, his voice more sympathetic than she'd ever heard it. "Why don't you take the rest of the day off? I am."

Katherine shrugged. And do what? she asked herself. She rarely called in sick, even when she really wasn't feeling well. That was the kind of thing undependable people did. Work, and the life she had structured around it, meant everything to her, even though she was by no means on a fast-paced career track. No, she was definitely trodding the slow lane of employment. But she was good at what she did, she reminded herself. It was a nice, stable, normal life.

She turned to leave his office.

"Mother of mercy!" Warren cried. "What have you gotten yourself into?"

Was it that obvious, then? Katherine wondered. Were her growing feelings for Homer written all over her face? She looked at her boss, but he wasn't staring at her face at all. Katherine twisted, trying to get a glimpse of where Warren's eyes were glued in horror.

"What did you do, sit in a soufflé?"

Nadine's éclair was a gooey mess on the back of her gray linen skirt, bringing back memories of what she had been doing when she sat on it. A little yelp of dismay escaped her lips, but it wasn't entirely about her ruined clothing.

# Chapter Six

Katherine aggressively avoided going home that night. She hadn't seen Homer since lunchtime, so she supposed he was still busy touring the Virginia plant. When he got back, he would have to check into the hotel where Mr. Warren had found him a room. She wondered if he had already gotten his clothes and things out of her apartment and thought wistfully of his all-in-one toothbrush.

She left the office at five, but she didn't go straight home. Instead, she walked toward Capitol Hill. Looking down the mall at the many Smithsonian buildings, she chose one at random and went inside.

But sitting in the lobby of the Museum of Natural History, she could only think of Homer and how taken he'd be with the enormous stuffed elephant near the building's entrance. Then she thought despondently about the empty apartment that awaited her.

It was an unproductive way of thinking. She loved her apartment, had always enjoyed going home there at night and curling up on her sofa with a good book. She got up and walked out of the museum, determined to enjoy her solitary evening. On the way home she purchased a gift for her fish—a new plant for their tank—and for herself an eight-hundred-page saga of a Bostonian family.

When she finally entered her apartment, she reminded herself again how much better off she was with Homer not there. The first thing she did was turn the stereo back to her classical-music station. While she planted her freshwater fern in the fish tank, she caught herself humming along with Vivaldi and stopped immediately. Humming was not something she'd normally done before she'd met Homer, and she was certainly not going to start now.

By the time she flopped down onto her couch, she was content to be getting back to her old way of life. It was amazing to her that a few short days could make her forget how much she'd always enjoyed her solitary existence. She stretched out and opened her book.

Then the noises started overhead. First, a series of thumps that didn't sound exactly like Millie. Katherine sat up, alert. Perhaps it could have been Millie if the puppy was extremely agitated. But that worried her, too. She momentarily debated going up to check on Gladys Hobbs—maybe there really was a burglar in the building this time. Then she heard a loud *blonk,* as if someone had fallen.

Katherine stared nervously at the ceiling. A sound like a slow *whish* made up her mind for her. There was no mistaking it—someone upstairs was dragging a body across the floor and that body could only be poor Gladys

Hobbs. With alarming quickness, Katherine was out her door, just stopping long enough to pick up her neighbor's keys and a vacuum-cleaner attachment, which was the closest thing to a weapon she could find in her mad dash to the elevator.

A lump formed in her throat at the thought of something terrible happening to Mrs. Hobbs. She had never cared all that much about the woman before Homer had come. But now, she remembered the many kindnesses Gladys had shown her, apart from the fish-sitting, and Katherine felt guilty for not recognizing the woman's better qualities earlier.

She leapt out of the elevator before its doors had opened completely, then ran hell-bent-for-leather to Mrs. Hobbs's. She inserted the key into the door, kicked it open, and the next thing she knew she was standing in the middle of the old woman's quaint room, with three pairs of round eyes staring at her as if she'd gone off her rocker.

Had she, or had they? There was nothing normal about the scene in front of her. Gladys and Nadine sat on the couch, their mouths open and their arms askew. They appeared frozen in midmovement, although what they were doing exactly was a mystery. Homer was flat on his stomach on the Persian rug, arms splayed out on either side of him. He smiled at her, handsome as ever, and she would have been overjoyed to see him had she not been so totally confused. What on earth was happening?

"It's Katherine!" Gladys finally broke the silence and got up from a chair to greet her.

"Am I interrupting something?"

"Not a thing in the world, honey. We're just playing charades."

Before Katherine could quite refocus, Gladys was piloting her toward the settee and seating her next to Nadine. She and Nadine exchanged greetings, but Katherine couldn't keep her eyes off Homer, his long muscular legs stretched out, his strong sinewy arms bulging against the material of his shirt. When she looked up, she saw that he was giving her that look again, that shameless, sexy, wanting look.

What was he doing here? she wondered. Why wasn't he at his hotel?

"We're so glad you dropped by," Gladys said, oblivious to the undercurrent between Katherine and Homer. "Now we can play teams! I get Homer—he's the best. Now, where were we?"

"Homer was doing a song, second word, second syllable." Nadine regarded Homer and then Katherine with a knowing smile.

As soon as all three women were seated, Homer continued rooting around on the Persian rug, which Nadine soon guessed correctly was "boar," which rhymed with "more," and it was just a few little words after that when Nadine blurted, "'That's Amore'!"

Darkened blue eyes met Katherine's brown ones, sending a thrill through her. And when Homer squeezed next to her on the settee, she could barely concentrate as her partner acted out *It Happened One Night*. Homer, too, was noticeably silent, but Mrs. Hobbs guessed the title of the film and was overjoyed.

"You young people wouldn't know that one. But when I was a teenager, Clark Gable was king!" she cried happily.

The evening was animated. Katherine found herself laughing uproariously as each person put their dignity on the line for the sake of acting out titles of songs, movies and books. Even she, who'd never played charades before, found herself mugging, contorting and getting totally carried away by the fun of it all. But Nadine, who was brave enough to try anything, was the star player.

They called it quits when everyone was unanimously pooped out.

"Brother, am I hungry!" exclaimed Nadine, collapsing in her tracks.

"Me, too," Mrs. Hobbs said. She looked decidedly worn out.

In the next moment, Katherine found herself doing the strangest thing. "Let's order a pizza," she suggested, not thinking about the time of night, her job, or the many cans of chunky white tuna in her kitchen. When she realized what she'd said, her eyes flew to Homer's. They were gleaming straight at her, his eyebrow raised sharply in disbelief—or was it amusement?

"There's a place right around here that I've been meaning to try," he said, his rich voice making Katherine's cheeks warm at the memory of last Saturday night. He stood, smiling, and grabbed her arm. "It'll be faster if we get takeout." He pulled Katherine to her feet. For a moment they stood facing each other, inches apart, wordless.

"Olives and pepperoni," Nadine suggested, nudging them toward the door. "I'll make a pot of coffee while you're out."

The night air was brisk. Once on the street, Homer offered Katherine his arm. She welcomed his warmth as they walked snugly down the sidewalk together.

"I thought they'd sent you to a hotel," she said.

"That bothered you?"

Katherine bit her bottom lip. This was where it got tricky. "Things would be less, uh, lively."

Homer felt as though his heart would explode in a million jubilant pieces. It was all he could do to keep putting one foot in front of the other, instead of taking Katherine into his arms and thanking her for this one cryptic hint as to her feelings. All day he had wondered whether he was getting through to her at all, but Katherine could sometimes be about as readable as a rock.

Now he at least knew he had made some kind of impression on her. And he was beginning to wonder why that mattered so much to him, why in the past three days all of his energies, which were usually expended on his paper and his inventions, had zeroed in on this one woman. A woman who didn't seem to want to like him very much when it came right down to it.

He could only suppose it was because she was a mystery, a challenge. Katherine seemed convinced that they were opposites, but that only intrigued him more. To Homer, nothing was as seductive as something that needed to be fixed. And by his book, Katherine's life could definitely stand some fixing.

"Less lively, huh?" he finally asked.

"Well . . ." Katherine was puzzled by Homer's subdued manner since leaving the apartment. He seemed pensive—just as he had on the night he'd made her ear socks. She wondered what he was dreaming up in that brain of his now.

The pizza place was tiny, so there wasn't much room to move around in while they waited for their order. Katherine walked over to a corner and leaned against the wall, right underneath a travel poster of Rome.

"You never did say what you did with the hotel room," she said.

Homer stood next to her. "I canceled it." He cast her a sly glance.

Katherine nodded, her stomach tight. He was staying. The news elated her and made her anxious all at once. Elation won out, though, piercing through her system like a drug. "I can hardly put you out on the street."

Homer smiled, triumph surging in his veins. She wanted him to stay; she had come as close as she ever would to admitting it. The next move was his.

He made it ten minutes later, when they emerged from the fluorescent glow of the pizza place into the lamplit streets. The night was brisk and beautiful, and Katherine's presence and the pizza's aroma hit his senses like a sledgehammer. When she turned to him with her honey-soft voice to thank him for the balloons he'd sent, it all became too much for him.

He anchored the pizza box on his hip with one arm and dragged Katherine to him with the other. He wedged her firmly against his chest, reveling in the feel of her soft body against his.

Things happened so fast Katherine's head spun. "Homer—"

He cut off her words with a deep joining of their lips. Even though he could only hold her with one arm, he was strong, and his kiss was astonishingly intimate.

"Way to go, bro!" a passing kid yelled.

Katherine leaned as far back as Homer's tight grasp would allow. "We're on the street," she said, dazed. Until she had heard the kid's shout, she had imagined that she was somewhere else—somewhere private, secluded.

"I don't care," Homer said. "Everywhere I am I think of kissing you."

His voice was urgent, warm, so harshly tender that it sounded completely at odds with the rush of traffic and street noise around them. Katherine looked around, then took two steps back. Homer pounced right after her. She was no longer in his arms, but her eyes were trapped in the intensity of his. She stepped back again and collided with a parking meter.

She'd had a plan for this evening, she chastised herself. She'd been going to tell Homer that things had gone far enough, that any furthering of the relationship between them was impossible. But that had been before she thought she'd never see him again. And when she'd found him in Gladys's apartment, she had forgotten about anything except about how incredibly sexy he was and how relieved she was that he hadn't disappeared from her life.

But that had been a mistake of the moment, and now it was more urgent than ever that she make her intentions clear. "You've got to stop kissing me all the time," she said.

"Why?"

Good question, Katherine thought. Tricky. She could hardly say, "Because I enjoy it too much." Maybe it would be best to steer him away from the kissing issue altogether. "I'm not looking for a relationship, Homer."

There, she'd said it. She only hoped he'd been listening, because she didn't know if she had the strength to say it twice.

"Me, either," Homer said.

Katherine stared blankly at him. What did he want, then—just to pester her? Free homey lodging? And then it dawned on her. Of course, people like Homer didn't gravitate toward commitment—they just gravitated. Obviously he'd decided he just wanted a quick tumble and had decided she would do. And she'd been worrying about a lasting relationship! The very idea was probably foreign to Homer Ludlum.

Well, she wasn't going to be anyone's tumble, either, although she didn't know how to say so flat out without making an idiot of herself. Luckily Homer spoke before she had to.

"That's the beauty of it," Homer said. "I wasn't looking for anything when I came here."

*And you're not getting anything, either,* Katherine thought. She crossed her arms and waited for him to go on. He looked a little perplexed at her lack of response.

"Don't you see?" he asked. "The best things in life aren't planned. They're spontaneous—like our trip to the zoo...like the way I'm beginning to feel about you."

Oh, brother! Katherine thought. If Homer believed he could convince her to take a roll in the hay by telling her it would be as much fun as an afternoon looking at a panda, he was sorely mistaken. It was time to put a stop to this entire matter.

"We need to get back," she said firmly.

"But I just wanted—"

Katherine held up her palm, stopping him. "No more," she insisted. "Whatever you're thinking is impossible, Homer. I'm sorry, I really am, because I do like you. I like you, but you're strange."

She started walking. Confused as he was, Homer could only follow behind, speechless. Somehow he didn't think Katherine had understood his meaning correctly.

He'd meant to tell her he hadn't come to Washington with the intention of falling head over heels for his hostess. Maybe it hadn't come out right. All he knew was that Katherine had reacted to his words as if he had offended her, and then she had called him strange.

Strange! Why would she think that? Perhaps she was disappointed in him because he didn't fit her idea of a Texan. Or maybe she was holding out for a man who cut a more macho figure than he did. Or suave. Well, he could certainly be macho and suave if the occasion called for it. And this, obviously, was such an occasion.

He stepped into the elevator behind Katherine, hatching plans like mad. Tomorrow would be a decisive day, he decided. He couldn't wait for tomorrow.

Both were glad when they finally stepped across the threshold of Gladys's apartment, although the two women seemed a little suspicious about the amount of time Homer and Katherine had been gone.

"Where did you get that pizza?" Nadine asked. "Baltimore?"

Katherine slept unusually late the next morning. But then, she'd had a late night. And in a completely masochistic show of independence, she had decided not to use Homer's socks on her ears to sleep. The city noises had nearly driven her insane, but those socks were a crutch, and she was determined not to rely on Homer Ludlum. He wasn't going to seduce her with earplugs or anything else.

When she got up—late—she discovered he was trying to do just that. The comics had been slid under her door. After Katherine hurriedly dressed, she followed paper arrows placed on the floor, which lead to the kitchen. In the oven, set on low, Homer had left scrambled eggs and bacon, toast and hash browns. On the refrigerator was a note: "See ya at the office—Long Tall Homer."

She scarfed down the hardy breakfast guiltily—she was already breaking her pledge—and sent up a silent prayer that Homer would remember to be at Warren's office at nine.

She herself didn't arrive until nine-fifteen. She tried to slip quietly into her office, but Warren was waiting for her there. He motioned for her to follow him down the hall.

"Jiminy Cricket," he muttered as he stood aside to let her precede him into his office.

Katherine stopped dead in her tracks, causing Warren to crash into her. She hardly noticed. She stared in astonishment at . . . *Homer?*

"Well, howdy, Kathy-girl," Homer drawled in the thickest Texas accent she'd ever heard. He crossed the room in two massive strides and started pumping her arm in a handshake as though he hadn't seen her for years.

He took off his Stetson and wiped his brow with a bandanna he'd pulled from his pocket. "Phew! Mighty hot out today, idn't it?" He hooked a finger around a belt loop in his jeans and leaned back, never taking his eyes off Katherine. Like Warren, she was speechless.

"Say, you're running a little late this morning, aren't ya?" Homer asked.

"I'm sorry about that," Katherine muttered, dropping into a chair.

Bill Warren sat down himself, nervously, and motioned for Homer to do the same. Homer obliged, swaggering over to a wing chair and easing down lazily. He stretched out his long booted legs and perched his hat on his knees.

Warren cleared his throat to speak, but he never got a chance.

"I was just tellin' ol' Bill here that you were one hell of a little hostess," Homer said to Katherine. "I told him flat out that you were in need of a hefty raise."

Blood rushed to Katherine's cheeks with lightning speed. Warren began to cough and Homer chuckled. "He didn't seem to take to *that* none," Homer added.

"Yes, well," Warren began with an effort, "Mr. Farlane is coming in today to demonstrate some of the possible uses of your reversible—"

"Who did you say?" Homer interrupted.

"Uh, Mr. Farlane, from product development."

"Far-lane?" The question came out of Homer's mouth in twangy syllables.

"That's right," Warren clarified.

"'Cause we had some Far-lanes down in Ludlum once, and they were a passel of thieving crooks. We had to kick Floyd Far-lane off the Ludlum school board."

"Uh," Warren began, "I don't think this is the same family."

Katherine had sunk so far down into her chair she thought she might melt into the upholstery. Unfortunately that didn't happen. Robert Farlane came in only seconds later.

Homer stood with typical Texas geniality and gave the man's hand a mighty shake. "Nice to meet ya, Farlane," he drawled. "Name's Homer Ludlum, Texas inventor."

Mr. Farlane, in his regulation blue suit and white shirt, smiled kindly, as if Homer's manner was perfectly normal. But Katherine wanted nothing more than to be shot and put out of her misery, and Warren seemed to be directing similar wishes toward Homer.

It took a few minutes to discern that the product manager was not one of the thieving Farlanes from

Ludlum. Then Warren promptly suggested they all adjourn to a conference room down the hall, where things had been set up for a presentation. Katherine sighed with relief because she wasn't expected to attend—but she wasn't off the hook yet.

As they were leaving the office, Homer turned to her, his eyes dancing with mischief. "Say!" he cried. "I never did tell ya'll how much I appreciated the special accommodations ya'll provided. That little lady has all the amenities, if you catch my drift." He laughed uproariously while the other three gaped at him.

"Didn't we provide Mr. Ludlum with a hotel room?" Mr. Farlane asked, concerned.

"Not until last night," Warren apologized.

"Yup—sort of like shutting the barn door after the horse is gone. Way gone, if you know what I mean."

Homer winked lustily at Katherine and slapped Farlane on the back. He hooted all the way down the hall.

No balloons were delivered to Katherine's office that day—just roses and violets, which arrived hourly. First came a box of twelve blood-red long-stemmed roses. The card read: "Roses are red. H." Simple, trite and completely unimaginative.

So that was his game, Katherine thought. Homer was obviously launching himself into the realms of normalcy—or his twisted conception of it. By eleven o'clock, flowers were stuffed in every available corner of her office.

Homer popped into her office at noon. "I'm taking the Boys out for lunch," he said, shutting the door and making a big show of taking his hat off in front of a lady. Knowing Homer, the gesture was something he would do, anyway, but in his big white Stetson and Colonel Sanders tie, it was comical.

"Am I getting to you, sweetheart?" he drawled.

"No, but I have a sneaking suspicion you're getting me a little closer to the unemployment lines."

Homer flopped into a chair next to the third round of roses, which had just arrived. "Hell, no, honey, I've told them fifty times this mornin' that you were due for a promotion."

Katherine rolled her eyes. "All right, Mr. Texas, you've had your fun. Just promise you'll give me a chapter in that book of yours when I'm down and out."

He reached over and, with a quick yank, pulled Katherine onto his lap. "I could write an entire book about you, sweetheart."

He bent down and covered her mouth in a swift ruthless kiss. Katherine saw it coming and knew she could evade his assault about as easily as a trapped fly could escape a sticky spiderweb. Even so, the feel of his lean muscles so close to her flesh, the pressure of his lips and the blatant desire she could feel swelling within him obliterated her thoughts of fleeing. With a soft whimper, she gave in to the growing warmth rushing through her.

That sound both aroused Homer and brought him back to earth—or office. God, she was something. If they hadn't been seated on a swivel desk chair, he didn't know how far they would have gone.

He brought them both up to standing and with the tip of his nose nuzzled the confused adorable wrinkles off Katherine's brow. "Ever heard of the Rodgers and Hart songwriting team?" he asked.

Katherine looked into his eyes through a haze of pleasure and confusion. Feelings like this were definitely out of place at work. "I guess so," she answered.

"They wrote a great little song once," he said, placing his hat on his head with a wicked grin.

Before Katherine could even ask what it was, Homer was gone. But she could hear him strolling down the echoing hallways singing, " 'If they asked me, I could write a book...' "

He sent candy, too, and the flowers just kept on coming. By the end of the day Katherine's tiny room looked like an FTD warehouse. She didn't know what to think. It was obvious that Homer was trying to romance her with a vengeance—probably because his time in Washington was drawing to a close. And she was surprised at how sad that thought made her.

Warren came by at five o'clock, looking beat. One glance at her office nearly sent him over the edge. "What on earth, Henry? The place looks like a hothouse!"

"I'm sorry, Mr. Warren," Katherine said. "It's Homer Ludlum again. I think he...has a crush on me."

"Oh, my God," Warren exclaimed, "the man's running amuck!" Then a wicked gleam came to his eyes. "Can we file harassment charges?"

Katherine shook her head. "I don't think the situation is that dire."

"I'd do about anything to get that guy off my chest." He lifted a vase of violets off a chair and collapsed. "I'm an old man, Henry."

"You're forty-five, Mr. Warren."

Warren waved a tired hand in the air. "Another day with Ludlum and I'll be ready for a nursing home."

One day. Was that all? Katherine pushed down the panicky feeling that jolted through her. The man wanted to have a fling, she reminded herself. She only had to fend him off for one more day. But somehow she couldn't drum up much enthusiasm for preserving her virtue.

"You know what that maniac did?"

"What?" Katherine was afraid to ask, but her boss obviously needed to talk about it.

"Both Wittington and Farlane were ready to take Ludlum to the best restaurant in town, and the guy puts up a big stink about it. So where do you think we went?"

Katherine shrugged.

"A soup kitchen! Can you imagine making the president of a prestigious corporation ladle soup to vagrants all afternoon?"

Katherine nodded sympathetically. But the strange thing was, she could imagine it, and she wasn't surprised at all. Or appalled. In fact, she wished she could have been there to see the president, the product manager, her boss and Homer Ludlum dressed like Roy Rogers all pitching in together.

What had Warren said just days ago? Something about presenting Homer Ludlum with a view of a corporation with a friendly face? It appeared it had taken Homer himself to do that. The thought made her laugh.

"What's so funny?" Warren snapped.

"Nothing," Katherine said, giggling.

"Good Lord," Warren said, throwing up his hands. "Everybody's going bonkers."

# Chapter Seven

Homer was no Valentino, but he could turn on the charm when he wanted to. Or at least he hoped he could. He had never really gone all out to wow a female, had never really seen the point. The last woman he'd tried to impress was Mary Lynn Baskin, but she'd been hardly worth the effort. Mary Lynn was a marriage-minded schoolteacher, and she acted the part.

Katherine was as different from Mary Lynn Baskin as night from day. Oh, Katherine put up a good front of being happy, being practical and stable, but Homer could tell a ripe melon from a mushy one just by thumping the rind. And he could tell that Katherine was a lot riper for adventure beneath that militantly staid exterior of hers than she dared let on. To be sure of this, however, he had to get close enough to thump her.

He had come damn close that afternoon, but that was just part of the charade. Or was it? Heaven knew Katherine made stooping to caveman tactics easy, as well as enjoyable. And after he felt her melt in his arms, it had been simple to spend the day with a toothy Texas grin spread all over his face.

Tonight, when he had her just a little off-balance, he was going to take her out for a real live, honest-to-goodness evening on the town—dinner, a show, maybe even some dancing. He didn't know if he would be able to stand so much normalcy. He certainly hoped Katherine wouldn't.

He knew it was a good sign when he opened the apartment door for her that evening in a suit and tie, and she looked at him as though he'd lost his mind.

"I didn't know what to expect," she said, peering over his shoulder as if hesitant to come inside her own place. "I was sort of afraid to come home."

"Get dressed," Homer said. "I'm taking you on a date."

"A what?" Katherine gaped at him. Then her eyes trailed down the length of his body, aghast. By the expression on her face, he might have been garbed in a toga, instead of his best suit, freshly pressed. "What are you wearing?" she asked suspiciously.

"A suit."

"What for?"

"Like I said, I'm taking you on a date. I made dinner reservations for seven. I hope that gives you time to change. The limo's picking us up at six-thirty."

*Limo?* Katherine clutched her purse stubbornly as Homer tugged her inside and shut the door behind him. "This is rather presumptuous of you," she said haughtily.

"I know," he agreed. "I've taken care of everything. I hope you like French cuisine and Italian opera—*Rigoletto*—because that's the agenda. And you'd better wear shoes you can move in, because we're going dancing afterward."

Katherine's jaw nearly hit the hardwood. "You're serious, aren't you?"

He took her arm and escorted her to her bedroom door. "You'd better hurry. I picked out a dress for you to save time, but we're still running a little late."

With an unceremonious shove, Homer pushed Katherine into her bedroom and closed the door after her. She stared at the low-backed emerald-green dress laid out for her on the bed. Tags still dangled from the sleeves and the belted waist. She had bought the silk dress on the spur of the moment, hoping that an ambitious wardrobe would reap a successful social life. It hadn't of course. And now she rued the frivolity of what she had done in a moment of weakness months ago. The elegant dress was suitable for the opera, but the back was impossibly low, and the full skirt suddenly seemed alarmingly feminine. Which was probably why Homer had picked it in the first place.

She sighed and stripped out of her gray work clothes. Nothing else she owned would be appropriate for what Homer had planned. Dinner. Dancing. The *opera?* What had gotten into him? His drill-sergeant-dream-date routine was overwhelming enough. But Homer, dressed in a tailored suit! Why, he looked almost...suave.

She would just have to accept it. Homer Ludlum was sexy—she would have to have been comatose not to have noticed that by now. And of course he was rushing her. He only had one day left to maneuver himself into her bed. Not that she was going to let that happen, she reminded herself firmly. French food and *Rigoletto* didn't necessarily buy a full night of romance. Although he did look awfully handsome in that suit....

Katherine didn't know what to do with her hair, so she put it in a French braid and tucked it under in the back. The style fit her dress. She dabbed on a little more makeup than usual—pink lipstick, blush and very light eyeshadow. Sitting in front of her mirrored dresser, brushing on a final touch of face powder, date adrenaline kicked in.

She was as nervous as a teenager on prom night. She herself had missed her own prom, so she was only going on hearsay, but she couldn't think of any other excuse for the butterflies in her stomach and the queer edginess that made her look at her watch every two minutes and hold her breath. With a laugh, she decided she was glad she'd been an unpopular teenager, if this queasiness was any indication of what she'd missed.

Homer waited in the living room, holding a clear plastic box with a pink ribbon around it. He was anxious. He kept thinking about that silky green dress with the tags still on it. He would be the first man on the planet to see Katherine in that dress, and his hormones couldn't forget the memory of the nonexistent back on that garment. He glanced toward the door for about the thousandth time, and it miraculously opened.

He shot off the couch and skidded to a quick stop in front of Katherine. She was beautiful; he couldn't tear his eyes away from her. She also looked terribly sophisticated, which made his case of nerves even worse. Her face was made up, and her hair looked like something straight off the cover of a magazine. He felt rumpled standing next to her, and the plastic box suddenly felt like a brick in his hands. This was not how he'd planned to start the evening at all.

"What's that?" Katherine asked, her gaze focused on his hands.

"It's for you," he said, handing her the box with the enthusiasm of a mailman delivering junk mail.

Some of Katherine's cool exterior dissolved as she took it from him. She inspected the thin plastic with wonder, as if she had never seen a florist's box before. Then she walked slowly past him and carefully seated herself on the arm of a heavy wooden chair. Her hand hesitated on the pink ribbon.

"You got this for me?" she asked, as though he'd made a mistake.

"Yes," he assured her lightly. Good Lord, he thought, he had been having flowers delivered to her all day long, and now she seemed about to faint over this single one!

She tugged at the ribbon, which fell easily into her lap. After pulling the top off the box, she looked down and gasped. "An orchid," she said reverently. "A white orchid."

Homer shifted uncomfortably, not sure whether to be pleased or not. He hadn't wanted to make her sad, which was how she looked sitting there staring at that flower like it had diamonds for petals. "Is it okay?" he asked. "I didn't know what kind of flowers you liked... I mean, I'm not really good with things like that..." He was stammering, so he decided to shut up.

She stood, her eyes bright, and moved toward him. She was holding out the flower as if she wanted to give it back to him. "I've never been given anything so beautiful."

"Oh." Homer puzzled for a moment. "Then why are you handing it to me?"

Katherine threw back her neatly coiffed head and laughed. "You're supposed to pin it on me." She chuckled. "Or at least I think you are."

There was a pin the size of a saber stuck in the stem, and Homer picked it out carefully. "Where?" he asked, scoping out her chest.

Katherine looked down the front of her dress. "I—I don't know. Wherever."

The orchid jittered in his hand as he looked for an appropriate place. The bodice of her dress was fitted, and even though he knew the damned flower didn't go there, he couldn't help looking at her breasts pushing against the rich fabric. He dragged his gaze a little higher, spotting a nice place below her collarbone, but as he leaned in, he was hit with an intoxicating blend of soap and soft perfume. His throat went dry. They were close, standing just in front of the bedroom door. It was only a little past six, and he wanted nothing more than to see her out of that green silk dress and in his arms.

He shoved the flower back into her hands. "We're a little late," he said hurriedly. "I'll feed the fish while you figure out what to do with the flower."

Homer sped around the corner and nearly collapsed against the aquarium. Lord, he was in way over his head. He had planned on feeling some discomfort during their first—and hopefully last—formal date, but this was too much. They hadn't even eaten yet, and already he ached for her.

He ached all the way to the restaurant, too. Sitting next to Katherine in a limo was a heady experience. Luckily their driver, Abdul, kept up a steady patter of conversation, or Homer didn't think they would have made it to the restaurant at all. Of course, that was Abdul's thinking, too.

"Mr. Homer," he railed, "why do you want to eat this French food? My cousin Ralph, he makes the best Lebanese food in town."

Katherine watched Homer carefully. It was typical of him to strike up an easy discussion with a D.C. limo driver in a matter of minutes, she mused. He just seemed to have the kind of face that drew people in. She was surprised how he stuck to his guns, though. Tonight he seemed determined not to stray from the itinerary he'd planned.

Abdul shrugged, muttered something more about his cousin Ralph's culinary skills and started talking baseball instead.

The restaurant was lovely, and Homer and Katherine stuffed themselves. Homer had even remembered that Katherine preferred corner tables to windows when he'd made their reservations. They talked easily, anticipating the opera, which Katherine discovered Homer truly loved.

The opera itself was harder to bear. Their orchestra seats seemed impossibly close together. All through the first act, Katherine found herself bumping against Homer's shoulder, his arm, his thigh. Each touch sent a jolt of electricity through her, and she was aware that they were tentatively watching each other as much as what was happening on stage.

Homer finally muttered under his breath and took her hand in his. They stayed that way until the curtain call, when Homer leapt out of his seat. He was a prima donna's dream, clapping and whistling and grinning like mad. He really did love the opera, Katherine thought, laughing, realizing she had missed his normal exuberance during their subdued dinner.

When the lead tenor emerged from backstage, Homer finally bellowed a heartfelt bravo and whistled frantically. In the frenzy of the multitude of excited Verdi fans, though, his reaction was not out of place. Katherine was buoyed by the crowd's energy and found herself letting out a few bravos of her own before the curtain went down for the final time.

Abdul was beside himself. When the driver had said he'd never been to an opera before, Homer had purchased a nosebleed-heaven seat for him when they arrived. Now Abdul was a fan, too, barely able to concentrate on the road.

"It's like we Lebanese say—*bonissima!*"

Katherine laughed and Homer wrapped an arm around her shoulder. His eyes were on fire with so many emotions—merriment, concern, desire. She felt them all, reveled in them, especially the delicious anticipation she could see in his eyes, which she knew mirrored her own. Her common sense was being undermined, and she knew it. And she couldn't wait to taste his lips on hers again.

"So where to now, Mr. Homer?" Abdul asked.

Homer gave him the name of a prominent downtown hotel. Abdul frowned. "Are you sure?" he asked.

Homer looked worried. "Is there something wrong?"

"With such a beautiful woman on my arm, I would wish for much more than big bands...."

Homer shot a quizzical look at Katherine, and she nearly exploded with laughter. "Where would you suggest?" she asked over Homer's protests.

Abdul's idea of the perfect place was a basement nightclub with a reggae band. Homer took one look at the tropically bedecked walls and the shaggy musicians and turned back to Katherine. "I don't want you to forget that we came here at your bidding."

"We did, didn't we?" Katherine said, scoping the crazed room in amazement as Homer steered her to a vacant wicker table. The constant merry thumping of the drum exactly matched the happiness in her heart.

Homer watched Katherine sip a daiquiri in her sexy green dress and sweated. She had never been more desirable. This threw a real wrench in his sedate evening. Her whole body seemed to be pulsating to the intoxicating rhythm, and it took every ounce of control Homer had not to leap across the wicker table and embrace her.

"Is something wrong?" Katherine asked, contentment written all over her flushed face.

"Everything." Homer muttered a curse and pulled her out of her chair and toward the dance floor. Katherine balked like a mule, digging her heeled pumps into the floor tiles. Despite her protests he tugged her along, and she skittered after him like a stork on ice skates.

In the thick of the crowd he grabbed her hips and pulled her to him. It was agony, but he couldn't help himself.

"I don't dance, Homer!" Katherine yelled above the music.

Homer grinned. Katherine hadn't realized it, but she was bobbing up and down to the infectious beat as surely as all the people bouncing and grinding around them were. "Look at yourself!" he hollered back.

Katherine gave him a puzzled glance and then looked down at her feet. They were moving. "You're right!" she cried, shocked. "I'm dancing!" She threw back her head and let out a primal whoop.

They danced for two hours straight. Katherine, once started, was tireless. To fast songs she bounced and laughed and undulated provocatively; to slow ones she

draped herself so intimately around Homer he thought
he would burst.

Later, Abdul treated them to a slow scenic drive
through Washington in the wee hours. The monuments
fairly glowed through the blanket of night. Joy so strong
welled up in Katherine that she wanted to roll down the
window and wake the whole city up to the splendor of
the night. Instead, she clung tightly to Homer's lapels
and stared out the limousine with rising happiness.

And fear. What now? she wondered. They would go
back to her apartment, and then... Yesterday the very
idea had outraged her, but what a difference a day made.
She'd never in her life had a love affair—although she
wasn't quite sure whether that was because of a lack of
will or opportunity—but snuggled next to Homer's
chest, the whole night yawning before them, she couldn't
say she was averse to the idea now. In fact, quite the opposite.

Homer nuzzled the crown of her head and she sighed
with pleasure. She was probably making the mistake of
her life, and she was thrilled. Homer's heart was
pounding away in his chest and she could feel the taut
power of his muscles, wound tight as a spring. She
wondered if he was thinking along the same lines she
was.

They bade Abdul good-night and walked arm in arm
to her apartment. The slow ride up the elevator was
passed wordlessly in mounting anticipation. She fum-
bled with her keys at the door and Homer took them
from her and opened it with a jerk.

Katherine stood in the middle of the room in a daze,
waiting for his next move. After a moment she noticed
that Homer hadn't looked at her since they'd entered the

apartment. Instead, he was rushing around at lightning speed, gathering his things together.

"What are you doing?" Katherine asked.

"Leaving," Homer answered, packing his shaving lotion and all-in-one toothbrush in the side pocket of his suitcase.

*Leaving.* The word was a thousand-volt shock. Katherine's whole body trembled. "You're what?"

"Leaving," Homer repeated. His heart fell when he saw her disbelieving expression. She looked so vulnerable—but that was precisely why he had to go. "I forgot to tell you. I've rented a room."

"At a hotel?" Katherine asked.

"At the Y."

It figured that Homer Ludlum would forsake the luxury of a modern hotel for the YMCA, Katherine thought. But then, maybe he was just going there to find more people to interview for that stupid project of his. He'd probably gone through all the down-and-out souls in her neighborhood in five short days, and now, his use for her finished, he was moving on. Their night on the town had apparently been his way of saying thanks.

Humiliation swept through her. His way of saying thanks had been one of the most incredible evenings of her life. She'd felt beautiful and desirable, but more than that, during her night with Homer she'd experienced a feeling of abandonment completely foreign to her. So foreign that she'd almost lost her head completely.

Obviously everything she'd felt had been one-sided. As he double-checked to make sure he had packed everything, Homer didn't look like a man overtaken by desire. No, Katherine thought, he looked exactly like what he was—a vagabond preparing to go on his own merry way. She'd seen her mother perform that over-the-shoulder room check a million times.

"I guess that's it," Homer said. He buzzed his suitcase over to the front door, then put the remote in his pocket and turned toward Katherine.

She stiffened her shoulders and crossed her arms. "Goodbye," she said.

Homer smiled. "Goodbye?" he asked. "I'll see you tomorrow."

"That's right. Tomorrow you give your answer to Patriot. And then you leave Washington."

Homer rubbed his chin thoughtfully. "Not necessarily. I might stay on for a couple of days. I still have some unfinished business, you know."

Katherine's heart skipped a beat. Then Homer clarified. "Nadine's fortune puffs."

"Nadine's what?" she asked, disgruntled that *she* wasn't his unfinished business.

"Fortune puffs. It's an idea I had that I think might help launch Nadine's career in the catering business. They're a cross between a cream puff and a fortune cookie."

As always, Katherine was diverted by Homer's inventive mind. "You mean, people would bite into a cream puff and find a wad of paper inside?"

"I'm still working out the kinks," Homer said. "You know what they say about one percent inspiration and ninety-nine percent perspiration."

In light of her disappointment with the evening's conclusion, Homer's jaunty mood grated on her nerves. "I don't think perspiring on the cream puffs will serve your purpose much. Sounds ninety-nine percent hare-brained to me."

Homer laughed and put his arm around her. She shrugged out from under it. "Is there something wrong?" he asked.

"No."

He looked at her, concerned. "Are you sure?"

"I'm tired." Katherine blurted out the first excuse that came to mind, although she knew she wasn't going to sleep a wink that night. But she was restless to be by herself again. Now that Homer was leaving, she just wanted to get it over with.

He took her hand in his and walked to the door. "I had a fun time tonight," he said softly.

Fun. The flimsy little word was devastating. "Me, too," Katherine gritted out.

He bent down to kiss her on the lips, and she turned her cheek to him. If the gesture bothered Homer, he certainly didn't show it. He straightened, turned the doorknob and went out into the hallway.

"Good night," he said.

Katherine smiled and watched him walk as far as the elevator. Then she ducked back into her apartment and closed the door. "Goodbye," she said for her own sake.

She collapsed against the door with a painful mixture of relief and frustration.

Homer tossed and turned on the squeaky bed at the Y. Katherine Henry was just about the most puzzling woman he'd ever met. It had taken every shred of gallantry he possessed to walk out her door tonight, even though she'd practically been pushing him through it.

He just didn't understand. Everything had seemed to be going so well between them at the nightclub, and then it all fizzled when they got to her apartment. He thought briefly of the look on her face when he'd told her he was leaving. Surely she understood why he had left.

Or maybe she didn't. Damn. He couldn't very well tell her that he would die of sexual frustration if he had to spend another night on her couch. It was either that or the Y.

Or seduction. He supposed he could have tried putting the big moves on her, but he didn't think that would have turned out too well, either. Not when just the previous night Katherine had told him she didn't even want to kiss him. Besides, he didn't want just a quick fling with her.

Oh, hell. Maybe he should have just explained how he felt about her. That he was falling in love. But there was no telling how Katherine would react to that news, either. In fact, if she didn't want to kiss him, she probably didn't want to hear him say he'd fallen in love with her, either.

He was in a terrible bind. Tomorrow he would wrap things up with Patriot, and then all that was keeping him here would be Katherine and a batch of cream puffs. Neither seemed much of a sure thing.

And then he had to get back to Ludlum. No telling what was happening with the paper. If he didn't return soon, they'd have to put out an entire edition of nothing but Ephram's obits. He tried to imagine Katherine in Ludlum—and then he remembered she'd been there already. She hadn't appeared to like it all that much. Not that she'd really gotten to see the place. It usually took a couple of decades or so for people to learn to love Ludlum.

Homer let out a bear of a sigh and flipped over onto his stomach. No matter how she might react, he would have to let Katherine in on how he felt soon. Tomorrow, he thought. Tonight he'd taken her on a date, but tomorrow he would get her alone and talk her ear off. He'd get down on one knee and beg her to come back to Ludlum with him.

Worry, something he wasn't normally prone to, rippled through him. He would have to make sure that everything went like clockwork tomorrow. And he prayed Katherine would be in a receptive mood.

## Chapter Eight

Katherine felt like strangling someone. Preferably Homer Ludlum.

This day was showing her just how difficult her job really was. She could type seventy words a minute, but every memo she wrote was agonizing. She had a naturally professional manner on the phone, yet today she found herself losing track of what the person on the other end of the wire was saying. She couldn't stop thinking of Homer; everything else that took up her time was an imposition.

It had been odd to wake up this morning without him there. There were no comics under her door, no arrows on her floor pointing the way to breakfast, no vague notes posted on her refrigerator. Her apartment seemed just as it had before she had ever heard of Homer Ludlum—sparse, spotless and empty.

Well, she thought philosophically, she could pat herself on the back for not falling for the guy—at least not too far. Even if she *had* fallen in love with Homer—and the very idea was preposterous—what would she have done? Moved to Ludlum? What would she have done about her life in Washington? She had a rent-controlled apartment, not to mention a thirty-gallon fish tank. A person just couldn't throw one of those into the trunk of a car and haul it across the country!

And in case she felt a little low in the months ahead, she would just have to remind herself of her long-held belief that everything would work out if she just stayed in the same place long enough. Putting her nose to the grindstone was always helpful, too. And somehow she would just have to force herself to forget all about how it felt to snuggle against Homer's strong chest and feel the thrumming of his heart—and know that she herself had made it beat just a little bit faster.

Only Warren's worse-than-usual crankiness late that afternoon brought her out of her melancholy stupor. Of course, that could have had something to do with the fact that he had just spent the day with the man she had spent the day thinking about.

"You got an aspirin?" Warren asked as he passed her office, and Katherine knew he must have news of Homer.

She got the bottle of aspirin from her top drawer and stopped only long enough to fill a paper cup with water. She was in her boss's office before Warren had even lowered himself into his leather swivel chair. When he struggled with the childproof cap, she whisked the bottle out of his hands and popped the top off, sending it flying and then rolling around the office floor. It finally landed under his desk, and Katherine got down on all fours to retrieve it.

"What's the matter, Henry? You seem jittery."

"Me?" Katherine asked, peering over the top of his desk.

"Of course you can't be any worse than I am after listening to that Ludlum character humming Italian arias all day. You think the guy has a split personality?"

Katherine donned her most sympathetic expression and eyed her boss innocently. "Is anything wrong?"

"Wrong!" Warren barked. "We've spent a whole week chasing after some hayseed inventor and he turned us down!"

"He what?" Katherine sank into her usual chair. She had half expected this, but the finality of it stunned her. The contract had been her first link to Homer—and was probably her last. Now the only thing standing between him and the open road were Nadine's cream puffs.

"That Ludlum character looked Mr. Wittington straight in the eye and told him he didn't like the way we were going to use his latch. Now isn't that a kick in the pants!"

Katherine frowned. "Just what had Farlane come up with that Homer found objectionable?"

"That's the clincher!" Warren cried. "It would have made the man a millionaire. We were going to use that latch on our first line of Patriot plastic semi-automatic toy guns—with retractable rubber bullets!"

"Oh, no." It didn't take a rocket scientist to understand why such a proposal wouldn't have appealed to Homer Ludlum.

"Can you imagine?" Warren snarled. "The man barely makes enough to keep a hick paper going!"

Katherine shook her head. She more than agreed with Homer's decision—and for once, she didn't feel like a traitor to her company. She only hoped that under the same circumstances she would have turned down the offer, too.

"Well," Warren grumbled as he swallowed his aspirin, "at least the guy's out of our hair."

Katherine sighed. "I guess so."

"Don't look so glum, Henry," Warren said. "There's good news, too. We have a deal practically wrapped up already with another guy who invented almost the exact same latch just for us."

Warren laced his fingers behind his neck and started whistling an Italian aria. All that trouble, Katherine thought, and the company had been working on copying the latch the whole time Homer had been in Washington. She shook her head in disgust and headed back to her own office.

To her surprise, Homer arrived at her office at five o'clock on the dot. He leaned lazily against her doorjamb, looking as if he owned the place.

Katherine scurried over, pulled him inside and quickly closed her door. "What are you doing here?"

"I came to pick you up," Homer said, a little confused by his reception.

Katherine tried not to react to his words with too much of a lift—but it was impossible. The day had been so gloomy and restive, and Homer looked genuinely happy to see her. Still, she tried at least to sound stern. "You're persona non grata around this place now, you know."

Homer shrugged. He was worried that Katherine would think his turning down Patriot's offer was foolish. In a way, it was. The company had offered him more for his latch than anyone else had. But semi-automatic toy guns . . . that had been the clincher. "The only person I'm concerned about around here right now is you."

Katherine's heart fluttered, then stopped. *Right now.*
The Homer Ludlums of the world lived for the moment, she reminded herself, then moved on. She couldn't let herself be built up, then given another letdown this evening. She could only enjoy Homer's company while it lasted.

"And all I'm concerned about right now is dinner," she replied, turning off her desk lamp and shrouding her typewriter with its plastic cover.

"You don't mind eating with a man who turned down a tidy fortune?"

Catching the anxiety in Homer's guarded expression, Katherine couldn't help herself. She smiled. "Mind?" she asked, eager to express her approval for what he'd done. "I'll even buy you dinner."

But at her urging, they left the building quickly, lest her boss spot her going out with his nemesis. The walk back to her apartment was spent amiably arguing over what to have for dinner, and somehow, somewhere along the way, their hands ended up intertwined.

Katherine didn't know how it happened, but that night her apartment was invaded. Gladys with Millie, Nadine, Homer and herself all gathered in the living room to witness the conception of the first batch of fortune puffs. Katherine had the sneaking suspicion that Homer welcomed the invasion, perhaps had even invited everyone to come down in the first place. Or maybe it had been spontaneous; people just seemed to spring up wherever he was.

"So how's things going with you two?" Nadine asked Katherine during a lull in the kitchen. She bobbed her red head in Homer's direction, where he was listening to Gladys.

"What do you mean?" Katherine asked, knowing and dreading Nadine's answer.

"I mean, are you two a couple or what?"

*Or what,* Katherine thought, but asked evasively, "Do we look like a couple?"

Nadine snorted. "Hon, I can spot people with the hots for each other a mile away. I lived on two things during my marriage—cooking shows and soap operas. And that's what you two remind me of. A soap. You, especially. You try not to pay any attention to him when you think someone else is looking. Soap-opera actors do that all the time."

Katherine blanched at the truth in Nadine's description. "I don't mean to," she said.

"Of course not," Nadine said. "You just want the rest of us to get the hell out of here. That's understandable."

"No, that's not true!" When Nadine leveled a skeptical glance at her, Katherine insisted, "It's not. Half the fun of the past few days has been having people around."

The words just slipped out, but once spoken Katherine realized how true they were. She *had* enjoyed herself, and she liked having people around her, too.

Nadine put a maternal hand on Katherine's arm. It really did look maternal, too, since Nadine had polished her long nails a red that resembled the Passion Red Marge had always favored.

"I never did thank you for what you did," Nadine said.

"Me?" Katherine asked, knowing instantly that Nadine was referring to getting her off the streets. "I didn't— I mean, it's Homer you should thank. And

Gladys." She was a little embarrassed to admit it, but she couldn't lie.

"I wouldn't have let my neighbors take in a homeless person, hon, and that's the God's honest truth. Not before I was one myself. Especially not an older woman like Gladys."

Just then, Gladys and Millie came bounding into the kitchen to check on the cream puffs. Katherine looked around her apartment in amazement. It was alive. Gladys Hobbs, who'd been just an upstairs neighbor a week before, was making herself at home in the small kitchen. Nadine, recently an unknown shadow on the way to work, now treated Katherine like a confidante. Even Millie seemed to be more than just a noisy mutt. Just mere days ago, Katherine would have looked upon the scene as an intrusion. Now it seemed more like family. And Homer was the tie that bound them all together. What would happen when he left?

In a sentimental, misty-eyed fog, Katherine moved toward the couch where Homer was sitting and flipping through a magazine. He put it down as soon as he saw her coming.

"Is anything wrong?" he asked. She looked incredibly sad.

"No," Katherine answered, "life just seems so wonderful." She sniffled.

Worried, Homer took one of her hands and cradled it in his. Was this Katherine talking? The world seemed topsy-turvy at the moment. The only thing he was certain of was what he wanted to say to Katherine—in private.

"Hey, folks!" Nadine bellowed from the kitchen. "Stop smoochin' in there. It's time to stuff the puffs."

Katherine jumped about two feet. "We weren't smooching," she defended. Then why did she feel as if they were? she wondered. Homer pulled a definitely sultry gaze away from her and lumbered toward the kitchen, and she followed close behind.

"I think Nadine was just joking, honey," Gladys said in a low voice as Katherine passed her. Even her neighbor seemed to have a sharper wit than her tonight, Katherine thought ruefully.

Her small kitchen was brimming with excitement, especially when it came time to put in the newly typed fortunes. They were trying all different kinds of materials to see which could best survive the cream filling. After all were done, they put the batch in the refrigerator to cool and retired to the living room for a raucous game of charades. It was almost ten o'clock when they finally checked on the cream puffs.

"Now we get to pig out!" Nadine cried, doing a little jig into the kitchen. She came out seconds later and placed the platter of pastries on Katherine's coffee table.

They decided that they would simply plunge in and eat their way through until they found a fortune-making method that worked. The first few tries were definitely disappointing.

"Oh, my goodness," said Gladys with a look of revulsion on her face.

"What happened?" asked Homer eagerly.

"I've just bitten into a mouthful of black cream." She held up the remainder of the cream puff. Sure enough, the typewriter ink from the piece of paper bearing the fortune had bled, leaving a trail of black goo in its wake.

"What about you, Nadine?" Homer asked methodically.

"Black goo."

Everyone had black goo, except Homer, whose fortune had been sealed with tape, imitating the laminating process they would no doubt have used when the demand for fortune puffs was so high they would have to crank them out by the dozens. But even so, he had to squeeze the cream off with his fingers before he could see what was written underneath. " 'Fortune puffs will be the hit of the catering business,' " he read aloud.

They had tried to use positive thinking when composing the fortunes for the first experiment. Now the optimistic words rang in the air with all the hopefulness of an off-key kazoo. Homer held up the slimy, sticky piece of paper for inspection.

"It doesn't look very appetizing," he said finally.

Gladys started to giggle. Nadine snorted. Seconds later the whole room was bursting with laughter. Millie howled at the riotous cacophony, which made everyone laugh louder.

It was only after the noise started dying down that Katherine became aware of the knocking. She immediately shushed everyone.

"I didn't hear anything," Nadine asserted.

"It's probably Mr. Bentley from the sixth floor," Mrs. Hobbs said, sniffing. "The man can't stand noise of any kind. Mavis tries to sneak music past him every Tuesday at bridge, but he won't tolerate it. I don't know how you've been able to live over him for so long, Katherine."

Because I never made any noise, Katherine inwardly moaned as she made her way to the door. She didn't like the idea of trouble with her neighbors. She'd been laughing as hard as everyone else, and now she felt guilty. Even a music-hating curmudgeon deserved to have peace. She tried to think of the words to apologize to Mr. Bentley.

"Hello?" she tentatively asked whoever was on the other side of the door.

"Hi!" answered a cheery woman's voice. It definitely wasn't Mr. Bentley.

"Who is it?" Katherine asked.

"C'mon, open up," the voice insisted.

"Who is it?" Katherine asked again. She had lived in the city long enough to know better than to open her door to a stranger, no matter how chipper—or oddly familiar—they sounded.

"Kathy-girl!" The annoyed exclamation sent a shock of recognition coursing through Katherine. "It's your mother!"

*"Mother!?"*

Instead of throwing the door wide in welcome, Katherine collapsed against it in shock. She knew it wasn't the polite thing to do, but it was instinctive. For a moment her gaze caught the other three in the room staring at her, completely nonplussed. Homer, especially, didn't seem to know what to make of her apoplectic reaction to hearing the news that there were only three inches of wood standing between her and her mother.

Finally, Katherine worked up the courage to open the door and stood face-to-face with her mother. Marge was still the same. She still wore her long, now graying brown hair to the middle of her back. She was dressed in jeans and a loose, gauzy Mexican-style shirt. Her face had virtually no makeup, but her nails still sported Passion Red.

"It's about time you opened that blasted door," she said curtly, giving Katherine a cursory hug. Marge quickly scanned the rest of the room, taking in the three sets of eyes focused on her. Her mood did an about-face at the welcome sight.

"People!" she exclaimed, moving into the middle of the group to introduce herself.

Katherine was shutting the door when she noticed Bo Welton, Marge's husband, still standing in the hallway. She motioned him in. Bo was a shy man, large and lumbering in a lovable way. Katherine had wondered more than once since their only meeting in the office of a Virginia justice of the peace why such a man would want to take on her mother.

Looking at him now, shyly moving into her living room after nodding to her briefly, she wondered anew what the odd couple saw in each other. Vagabonds, she decided. They come in all different varieties, but they can sniff each other out like skunks in a rosebed.

Marge had already snuffed down a cream puff by the time Katherine joined her guests. "Why, these aren't bad at all," she heard her mother say. "A little ink never hurt anybody! Try one, Bo."

Bo took the cream puff and started munching on it mechanically while the others watched him. Katherine, perched on an uncomfortable stool in the corner of the room, looked at Homer. He seemed perfectly calm. Calm, while she was a nervous wreck. His bemused expression annoyed her.

"Kathy-girl," her mother chided, "you never told me you had friends."

What was she supposed to say? That she didn't until last week? Katherine plastered on a bland smile and nodded.

"Why, every time I talk to Katherine," her mother continued as if her daughter weren't seated ten feet away, "she always makes out that her life is as dull as dishwater. Well, she never was popular in school, so that never surprised me. And here I come for a surprise visit, and Kathy-girl's having a party!''

Marge became so animated while she was telling everyone what a dull person her daughter was that Katherine thought she was going to sink into the floor. Her mother went on to describe some incidents in Katherine's childhood—including a particularly humiliating one involving a boy named Timmy, which Katherine didn't want to think about herself, much less have everyone else know.

"Mother..." she moaned, drawing jeers from the rest of the crowd.

"Oh, honey," her mother countered, "that was years ago! Besides, it looks like you're doing okay with the menfolk now."

She looked pointedly at Homer and emphasized the word "now" in a way that made Katherine want to disappear into thin air. Good grief! Her mother was embarrassing her more tonight than she had when she was an adolescent.

"What are you doing here, Mother?" Katherine asked casually.

"Oh!" Marge clapped her hands together. "Bo, can you believe I forgot to tell them?"

She referred to "them" as though everyone in the room was family. And to Marge, they probably were.

"So tell 'em now," Bo said.

"We're on our way to Europe!" Marge let the words ripple through the room like sunbeams. Nadine and Gladys "ooed" in just the right way, while Homer fixed a quizzical gaze on Katherine. He obviously wondered why she wasn't duly welcoming the news.

"For how long?" Katherine asked.

"Who knows?" Marge said with a complacent shrug. "Bo and I were driving through Tennessee, listening to some Memphis radio station, when they said they'd give a trip to Europe for anybody who could name the song that won the 1940 Academy Award. Remember when I took you to see *Pinocchio*, Kathy-girl, and you were so annoyed because I kept singing 'When You Wish upon a Star' all those weeks afterward? Well, I just knew that was the winning song, so I made Bo pull over to a pay phone, and we won!"

"So how long are you going to be gone?" Katherine asked again.

"What do you think, Bo? Three months? Three years?"

Bo shrugged. Katherine winced. "Didn't they give you a return ticket?"

Marge winked. "We're just hoping we won't have to use it."

Gladys told of her and Frank's trip to Scandinavia that they took in the fifties, and how they didn't want to come home, either. Not with all those beautiful tulips around them.

"We're probably going to stay a few months in Scandinavia," Marge said.

Katherine rolled her eyes. Even so, she felt a pang of envy and even a little excitement for her mother's good luck and coming adventure. "But how are you going to live?" she couldn't help asking, effectively squelching the dangerous twinges of camaraderie.

Marge waved a hand in the air. "Oh, we'll get by." Katherine noticed a fleeting look of apprehension cross her mother's face. "We do have a favor to ask you, though."

Uh-oh. Katherine's stomach knotted. "What?"

"Would you mind looking after Bo's rig?"

Surely she hadn't heard right. But the sudden gnawing in her stomach and the dead silence in the room told her she had. Katherine took a dry gulp and closed her eyes. "Did you say, Bo's rig—as in truck?" she asked quietly.

"That's right," her mother said cheerfully. "It'll just be for while we're gone."

Small comfort, Katherine thought, since her mother had just intimated that they might stay in Europe till the cows came home.

"I'd be much obliged if you just started her up and gassed her a little every once in a while," Bo said, obviously reluctant to leave his pride and joy.

Katherine couldn't believe her ears. "You mean you want me to keep it *here?*" she squeaked.

"Where else?" her mother said. "We went to the trouble of driving it all the way up here."

"*Here?*" Her voice approached a shriek. She couldn't imagine how such a mammoth thing could have made it into the city. She was sure it was illegal.

"I'm afraid Bo had to double-park."

Five minutes later, they were all gathered around Bo's rig, double-parked on the main avenue in front of Katherine's building.

"My," Gladys exclaimed, "it sure is big!"

It was a monster. Like one of those creatures out of fifties' horror movies, come to devour Washington, D.C. Or at least Katherine's small part of it. The big forest-green cab loomed frighteningly bright in front of the steely cargo area, which, to Katherine's stunned eyes, seemed to stretch for blocks. She felt her knees go weak at the thought of baby-sitting the god-awful thing, and then she felt a firm hand supporting the small of her back. Homer's hand.

"What are you going to do with it?" he murmured.

"I don't know," she whispered, but she was so short of breath she wasn't even sure if her words were audible. At least Homer had the good sense to see the gravity of the situation, she thought. There was a crowd gathering around the huge truck, and angry cars honked as they veered around it.

"We've got to get some of these cars out of the way," Katherine heard Marge say testily, "so we can park it right."

Katherine was nervous about leaving her apartment the next morning for fear of what she might find there when she came back that evening. She could very well imagine her mother seeing the apartment as her own new home and deciding to repaint—she didn't even want to think about what colors Marge might choose. She edged past Marge and Bo, zonked out on the couch, and grabbed an inky cream puff before dashing out the door for work.

She almost tripped over Homer as she tore out of the building. "Oh, it's you," she said when she recognized him.

Homer handed her the comics, but in her present state, it took her a few moments to register the gesture as a friendly one. "I'm sorry," she said, finally taking the proffered newspaper. "I'm so worried about my mother I can barely think about anything else this morning."

Homer frowned. "What's the matter with her?"

Just then, Katherine caught sight of the truck looming in front of her. She let out a gasp. For a while, she'd hoped she'd simply been having a nightmare. But no, the truck was there, she noticed, decorated with angry and official-looking yellow slips.

"It might be towed out of your hands," Homer quipped, trying to ease her worry. He didn't know what to think of Marge, or Katherine's attitude toward her, but the relationship was obviously a strained one. Katherine was as jumpy as a grasshopper this morning.

"Now wouldn't that be great!" she exclaimed in response, throwing up her hands.

"It'd certainly solve all your problems."

"No, Homer," Katherine lectured bitterly. "That . . . that *thing* is my responsibility now. I just can't let it get towed away. You would say something like that."

"Take it easy. It's not a sure thing the truck will be towed. And maybe," he suggested, "I can find a place to keep it."

"I'll do that myself," Katherine said tersely. "But thanks."

"Let me do it. I have time on my hands."

His voice had a soothing effect on her nerves. He was trying to help her. She didn't have to face the next day with her mother alone, she realized. Marge's plane didn't leave until the next afternoon. Katherine would need all the help she could get, and all the moral support.

"I'll give you my keys," she said. "That way, you can use my phone to call places, instead of the pay phone at the Y." And maybe, she hoped, he wouldn't let her mother paint her apartment garish pink, either.

Katherine spent an agonizing, nail-biting eight hours at work. When she called her apartment to see how things were going, she discovered her mother had changed the message on her answering machine. Her old businesslike message had been replaced with music and her mother's cheery voice telling callers about all the exciting things going on in Katherine's life. The storm-window salesmen would love it, Katherine thought, fuming.

Apparently no one was there in her apartment to take the call. And that worried her. She left a message for Homer. She didn't know why, but his was the first name that came to mind.

Homer called her office later. "Where have you been?" she barked.

"Oh, we did some sightseeing," he said.

"Have you gotten rid of the truck?" Katherine asked.

"Uh, not yet. Your mother said..."

Katherine groaned. Marge wasn't going to like her getting rid of Bo's truck. But it had to be done. Even if Katherine had to wait until Marge was in Luxembourg to do it. She told Homer as much—not that it was his business, really—and hung up the phone. The day was endless.

Homer was beginning to see why Katherine had become so root-bound. After a day with Marge, he was pooped. The woman had said she wanted to see every monument and point of interest in the city, and they practically had. Bo had lumbered along, just happy to be there.

At dinner that evening in a Chinese restaurant a couple of blocks from Katherine's apartment, Homer was surprised that Marge seemed oblivious to her daughter's feelings about her childhood. She reminisced the whole time about how much fun the two of them had always had. From the way Katherine twisted her napkin and refused to look up from her wonton soup, Homer guessed that Marge wasn't giving them the whole story.

"Remember, honey," Marge asked, "how you wanted to join the circus one summer?"

Katherine replied that she didn't.

"Oh, yes, you do! It was in St. Louis, and we went to see the circus. And you said, 'Mama, why don't I see if I could stay behind with these people?' Well, I'd always wanted to join the circus, too! And I told her there wasn't any better way to see the country than from a circus train, but then it turned out she didn't know that circuses traveled. I remember telling her about how they fold up their big top and pack everything in crates and hit the road, and the poor thing upchucked her cotton candy and said she wanted to go home. You never mentioned joining the circus again after that, did you, hon?"

"No."

"I didn't think so. Kids are funny like that—their minds just seem to wander and wander. Right after the circus, Kathy-girl decided she wanted to be a lighthouse attendant, so we went up and down all the coasts looking for lighthouses. And then she never once mentioned lighthouses again after that summer."

"That was two years after the circus," Katherine said flatly.

"Was it?"

Katherine seemed to remember their roving life-style better than Marge did, as though she'd been reliving every turn-off and stretch of road in her mind for years. In fact, she'd probably been doing exactly that, Homer decided, recalling her horror when he'd suggested driving to Washington the week before.

Did she think of him in the same light as Marge? If so, he was in serious trouble. While Marge was perpetually on the move, he was a man with a mission. He only hoped that Katherine realized the difference. He couldn't help laughing, though, at Marge's stories of Katherine, the practical one even as a child.

He walked back with them to Katherine's building.

"I know, Katherine," Marge suggested as they entered the apartment, "why don't you show Bo and Homer your photo album?"

"Oh, I couldn't," Katherine protested.

"I'm sure both men would love to see it."

Bo sat on the couch and studied the toe of his shoe, and Homer seemed to move instinctively to Katherine's side, a protective arm slipping around her waist.

"Well," her mother amended, "I'm sure Homer wants to see it, at least." She winked, and Homer cringed.

Katherine stiffened, then relented. "Oh, all right." She retrieved the large album from the top shelf in her closet.

"I bet you didn't even know my daughter's a shutterbug," Marge said, taking Homer's arm and leading him to the couch.

The four of them squeezed together to look at the pictures. They were all of Marge, wearing various outfits and expressions, in front of a grab bag of settings. Next to a picture of Marge in front of Old Faithful was a picture of Marge standing by a nondescript door with a number on it.

"What on earth was that?" Marge asked.

"That was the motel outside Vegas," Katherine replied, in a tone that said she'd recognize that door anywhere.

"How do you know that?"

"Mother, we spent three months there—look at the number."

The number was thirty-one. "Oh, I remember!" Marge exclaimed. "I kept telling you it was a good omen because we moved in the day you turned thirteen— thirty-one backward."

"I sure didn't make it to fourteen in that place."

Marge frowned. "Of course not. You can't stay in a motel for a full year. People would think you were some kind of kook."

Katherine grimaced and Homer squeezed her arm. "Why don't we go for a walk?" he said to her. After his day with Marge, walking was actually the last thing he wanted to do. But he did want to be alone with Katherine.

Katherine slapped the album shut and snatched a jacket from the closet. She was out the door in no time, moving faster than Homer had ever seen her go.

"Those pictures looked professional," Homer said when they emerged from the building.

Katherine laughed. "Hardly. Although I did become adept with a thirty-five millimeter. It was how I cataloged all the places I'd been."

"I can see how you missed having a home." He put an arm around her shoulders. She leaned into him slightly, which gave him courage. He cleared his throat inaudibly and said, "It wouldn't be like that for us, you know."

Katherine froze. Even with the traffic whizzing by, Homer swore in that instant he could have heard a pin drop. "Us?" Katherine asked.

Homer nodded, realizing suddenly that this wasn't a discussion that should be taking place on a busy sidewalk. If he got down on bended knee here, all he was likely to get were jeers from passersby and gum on his pants. And Katherine was looking anything but receptive. Still, now that the word "us" was out in the open, hanging between them like a near-to-bursting thundercloud, he couldn't pretend he hadn't said it.

"You and me," he pressed on. "If we just happened to wind up married somehow, I'd see to it that we had a permanent home. Maybe two or three."

Katherine stared at him, her mouth agape. *"Married?"*

It was do or die. Little beads of sweat popped out on Homer's brow. He could feel them. He just hoped they weren't visible to Katherine. "Married," he said again. "It's what people do when they're in love."

For long seconds, Katherine said nothing. Just stared at him. Homer couldn't quite figure out what to do next. What if she never said anything? They'd be stuck all night in front of the building, staring at each other. He shoved his hands into his pockets and opened his mouth to speak.

"Wait a second," Katherine said, cutting him off. "Let me get this right—are you saying you're in love with me?"

If she'd asked him if he'd said he had leprosy, her tone might have been the same. She looked horrified. Her eyes, round as saucers, blinked disbelievingly, and she stood stock-still, as though if she moved he would attack her.

"Yes," Homer admitted in a scratchy voice. "I'm in love with you, Katherine."

Katherine knew it was cruel, but she'd had to hear him say the words. Homer Ludlum looked more adorable in that instant than she'd ever seen him. The anxiousness in his deep voice, his earnest eyes, even the fine beads of sweat on his brow, made him seem so vulnerable . . . so lovable. But she didn't love him, she reminded herself.

She couldn't—all she had to do was glance over his shoulder to see the reason why not. Bo's rig stood as a warning to all persons considering an association with a vagabond.

"You've only known me a week," she countered, on one hand trying to talk him out of his feelings while on the other hoping he'd stick to his guns.

"It took me less than three days, Katherine, maybe just three hours, to know how I felt."

"Well, I'm a little slower," she said, glancing at the eighteen-wheeler again to build up her nerve. She couldn't string him along. "Frankly, I don't think I'd be sure about you in three decades."

That hurt. Homer knew she was thinking of her mother, not him. "I'm not Marge, Katherine. I have a permanent residence."

"Like your own mother said, Ludlum is just a jumping-off place to you."

"It's my home. I've lived there all my life. How much more permanent can you get than that?"

"That's not the issue," Katherine moaned. "I'm not like you. You like moving around and meeting people."

"You enjoyed meeting people this week. You told me so yourself last night."

"One week. For you that may be a significant amount of time, but for me a week is a week. It takes a whole lot of them to make a lifetime, Homer."

"I know that," he said irritably. How could he defend himself? What she said was true, but exaggerated. He feared that everything she expressed right now would be colored by her relationship with her mother. "I'm not like your mother," he repeated.

"You sure enjoy her company," Katherine said. "You two seem like birds of a feather to me."

"That's not true. A day with that woman plain tuckered me out—I can just imagine how you must have felt after eighteen years."

"You laughed at her stories about me. I saw you, Homer," Katherine insisted when he appeared completely dumbstruck. "She told that story about the circus and you chuckled. Admit it."

"It was a funny story," he pleaded.

"Not to me, it wasn't."

"I know that. And I'm sorry. But that's why it was funny—because your mother has no idea how you feel. Have you ever tried telling her you had a miserable childhood?"

"Of course not," Katherine said. Then she added, "I've never seen her long enough to talk about it."

"She's up there right now," Homer said. "And she'd probably be able to help you get over this fanaticism you have with stability. Life is too short—you can't spend half your time worrying that the people you love are going to leave."

Katherine's cheeks felt on fire. What had happened? One minute Homer was professing his love and the next he was lecturing her as if she were some kind of numskull. *Fanaticism?* Was this the word of a man in love?

"None of this is any of your business."

"I want to make it my business." Their eyes met briefly, and then, unexpectedly, he enfolded her in his arms.

Katherine gasped as their bodies collided. He cut off any protest with a stormy kiss, tender yet challenging. She thought for a moment of telling him just what she thought of his domineering attitude, but that was before her body melted against his sturdy warmth. He finally pulled away, but didn't let her go quite yet.

"That doesn't change a thing," Katherine said—as casually as she could when her heart was fluttering like mad.

Homer's blue gaze was piercing. "I've said I love you. I want you to marry me. Are you saying that doesn't change anything?"

Katherine took a step backward, out of his reach. He didn't want an affair, then; and his professing love wasn't just a whim. He wanted happily-ever-after. But after what? Katherine wondered, staring again at the truck. Homer Ludlum would be forever after the next story, the next invention, the next road trip....

She had worked so hard to make her life just the way she wanted it. Her apartment, her job, her very existence would change if she threw in her lot with Homer. The future would be an unknown. She couldn't give up the life she was leading for something so unsure.

"No," she said finally, sadly, "it doesn't change anything. It doesn't change who we are, Homer. You say I'm fanatical about stability. I think you're a rootless wanderer. Even if we're wrong, just our perceptions of each other are enough to make us incompatible."

"Perceptions?" Homer asked, growing angry. How was he supposed to get through to this woman? "I'm offering you my life, and you're talking perceptions?"

"That's just it, Homer," Katherine argued. "You're offering me your life as a better alternative than mine."

"It is!" Homer said, frustrated beyond reason. He knew he shouldn't be yelling in public at the woman he loved, but dammit, she was wrong.

Katherine threw up her hands. "I rest my case."

"Katherine." Homer took a deep breath. He had to stay calm. But it was difficult, because the more stubborn Katherine became, the more he felt his future hap-

piness slipping away. "I'm in love with you," he said
again. "I think you're in love with me, too."

"I'm not," she denied flatly. The words came out so
quickly, so surely, that Homer felt them like a slap.

Maybe *he* was wrong, he thought with dawning fear.
It had never occurred to him that Katherine liked her life
exactly as it was. Everywhere he looked, he saw things
to fix, to make better. But maybe she really had seen his
entrance into her life as an intrusion.

"Katherine..." He wanted to restate his feelings,
maybe couch them in terms she would accept. Katherine stood in front of him, arms crossed, jaw clenched in
determination. She didn't want to hear what he had to
say, that was for sure; and now that he thought about it,
he didn't feel like making more of a fool of himself.

He looked around. They were still on the sidewalk just
outside Katherine's building. Some walk, he thought—
the shortest, longest one he'd ever taken.

"I'm sorry for bothering you," he said. "But I still
think I'm right."

Katherine looked up, surprised. "Right about what?"

Homer took his hands out of his pockets. "About
your being in love with me." Her chin jutted out a frac-
tion more, and Homer gave up hope of changing her
mind. "I'll probably be going back to Ludlum, I guess."

Katherine nodded. What else could she do? She supposed this was her cue to throw herself into his arms and
say that she'd changed her mind about everything, that
she'd been waiting all her life for him. Well, she hadn't.
He'd just been tossed at her unexpectedly, like a curve
ball.

In phys ed, on softball days, she'd always wondered
at girls who would dive, leap or give their right arm to
catch whatever was thrown their way. If somebody hap-

pened to throw something that Katherine knew she couldn't handle, she simply ducked. She did that now.

She didn't actually duck; shrugged was more like it. The gesture wasn't the definitive statement she would like to have made, but somehow words wouldn't come. He was leaving. She'd always known he would. Things would be fine in about a month or a millennium or so.

"Well," Homer said, not moving, "guess that's it, then."

Katherine nodded. "Guess so," she said. Her voice was barely a whisper. He continued to look at her, and she tried to memorize how his eyes bore into hers, how tall he was, how the corners of his mouth just naturally seemed to turn up in a genial smile—even now, when she herself felt as if she was about to burst into tears.

She couldn't cry, not now. And they had to stop staring at each other. In an effort to put an end to the agony, she thrust out her hand awkwardly.

Homer stared dazedly at it. A handshake? He felt as if he'd been kicked in the gut. Still, his hand reached out and clasped hers. For a moment, he considered pulling her into his arms again. But he thought better of it; best to make a clean break.

"Goodbye," he said.

"'Bye," Katherine said.

Homer turned slowly and began to walk down the street. Katherine watched his figure receding with growing panic. Suddenly she sprinted a few yards and called his name.

He pivoted, a questioning look on his face.

It was comforting just to see that expression, but after a few moments Katherine realized she'd have to say something. "What about Nadine's fortune puffs?" she asked. They were the first words that came to mind.

"They still need some fine-tuning. I'll get in touch with her before I go."

"Go where?" asked Katherine.

"I'm not sure."

"Oh." They stared at each other for a few more moments, then Homer, with a sad smile, waved goodbye and continued walking away.

When he turned the corner, Katherine started back toward her building. She couldn't go in, though. There was no way she could face Marge and Bo when she felt as if all the air was being squeezed out of her lungs.

Katherine looked around. The only place she saw to wait out her misery was Bo's truck. She walked over and sat on the step leading to the cab.

She should be happy, she thought. Homer was gone. Tomorrow her mother would leave, too. All she'd have to contend with after that would be the truck. She'd made the right decision in turning Homer away.

She had. She'd made the right decision.

A single tear fell down her cheek.

## Chapter Nine

For the first time in the entire four years she'd worked for Patriot, Katherine called in sick when she actually felt fine.

At least, she didn't feel ill, exactly. But how was she supposed to concentrate on work when it was all she could do not to droop around as though she'd lost her best friend? It would have been an unproductive day, she told herself, and besides, she had to take her mother and Bo to the airport.

Yet she knew she wasn't obligated to escort them. Marge was one person who was certainly happy going it alone. Nevertheless, to force her mind off Homer and to get herself into the spirit of things, Katherine found her subway map and started plotting out the way. Then, as if to undermine her good intentions, a limo service called to say that one of their drivers would pick them up at two o'clock and take them to the airport.

"What?" Katherine asked the man on the phone. "I didn't call for a limousine."

Just then, Marge scurried over and took the receiver from her. "That'll be Abdul, Kath. We met him at his cousin Ralph's restaurant the other day."

"Oh," was all Katherine could say as she stepped aside and let her mother take over. She folded the subway map and put it back into the drawer.

All the way to the airport, she longed to be at work. At least there her mind might have been challenged enough for her to stop thinking about Homer. In the limo, with Marge and Abdul chattering away about him, it was impossible. Katherine kept her gaze focused on the passing scenery; the interior of the limo brought back memories of two nights ago—memories best left untapped now.

The wait at the airport wasn't long. Marge had just finished rushing around buying magazines and breath mints for the eleven-hour journey when their flight was called.

"That's us, Bo!" Marge cried. She was the first person in line at the boarding gate.

Katherine hurried after them. Now that the time had come, she wasn't sure she was ready to part with her mother. "Do you have everything? You have your passports, don't you?"

To her surprise, when Marge turned around, there were tears in her eyes. "Kathy-girl, you sound just like a mother. You're such a worrywart!"

"I just don't want you to—"

Before she could finish the sentence, she was engulfed in a gigantic hug. Her face was squished against Marge's batik scarf, her senses overwhelmed by the smell of perfume. "Don't worry," Marge said. "Bo takes as good care of me as you always did."

"As *I* did?" Katherine pulled away slightly, so she could see her mother's face.

"Of course!" Marge said. "I couldn't have gotten by without you, honey. But now I'm just glad you've found yourself that sweet Homer person to settle down with."

"But Homer—"

"I know," Marge said sympathetically, "Ludlum, Texas, would scare me, too." She clamped a Passion Red nailed hand on Katherine's shoulder and admonished, "But honey, if you get bored, you just make Homer take you on a trip. In fact, you two should come visit Bo and me in Europe!"

Katherine blinked, amazed as always at the Marge's-eye-view of things. "But, Mother—"

The attendant at the gate started taking boarding passes, and Marge gave Katherine another quick hug. "Stay sweet, honey, and let me know what happens." She shifted her purse and carryon bag, and began to sidle away from Katherine. "Life is so exciting!" She laughed as she passed through the gate.

Bo shuffled after her, smiling sheepishly. "I'll send a check for the parking tickets," he said. He patted Katherine's arm and disappeared through the long hallway leading to the plane.

Katherine stood in the terminal long after they were both gone, long after the plane had taken off, thinking about all the money she'd saved over the past four years living on tuna fish in her rent-controlled apartment. There was probably enough in her bank account to cover a plane ticket to Europe....

But she couldn't do that. She had a job; she had responsibilities. Yet suddenly those goldfish seemed more like a millstone around her neck than a reason to stay put. And another four years of tuna, nights at home

reading and Patriot Games and Toys loomed unappeal-
ingly ahead.

What was the matter with her? For the second time in
twenty-four hours, she'd stood by and watched as the
people she loved most in the world walked away from
her.

Katherine straightened. *Loved?* Homer?

Her brows knit together. She *was* in love—nothing else
could explain this anxious, lonely and empty feeling inside her. Why else would she be standing in an airport
terminal, contemplating escaping to Scandinavia? She
was in love, and she'd denied it both to Homer and herself. And she'd just stood there and watched as Homer
had left.

Katherine walked out of the airport in a daze. Of
course other people would always seem to be on the
move to her, she realized, when she was completely immovable. Life wasn't just passing her by, it was whizzing by, and she wasn't doing a thing to keep up with it.

"Home?" Abdul asked when she eased into the limo's
back seat.

At first she thought he'd said Homer—his name was
on her brain. Then it dawned on her what her next step
should be. She needed to get to Homer, if he was still in
Washington. "No," she replied. "I need to go to the
YMCA—as fast as possible."

"Okeydokey," Abdul said, and they were off.

Please, please, she thought all the way back into town,
let Homer still be there. At the Y, she sprinted out of the
car and up the stairs. But the man at the desk said that
Homer had gone.

Gone. She was too late.

She went back to the limo and told Abdul to take her
home. The driver, sensing her despair, said nothing, and
all the way back Katherine brooded over what to do

next. The only course of action left at this point was writing to him in Ludlum. She had to explain, let him know she realized how wrong she'd been about everything all along. But how was she going to sit still while she waited for a reply?

At her building, she said goodbye to Abdul and went up to her apartment. Her spirits were sagging a little, but she was determined to follow through with her plan. She was scouring her drawers for notepaper when her doorbell sounded. Katherine flew to the door, almost tripping over the coffee table, and threw it open. But it was only Nadine.

"That glad to see me, huh?" Nadine asked, taking in her expression.

"I thought... I mean, come in," Katherine murmured.

Nadine sashayed through the doorway carrying a plate covered in foil. "And here I thought you'd be all excited about the new improved fortune puffs."

In spite of her disappointment over Nadine's not being Homer, Katherine felt her stomach rumble hungrily at the mention of food. She hadn't eaten all day.

"I'd love to sample one," she managed to say with some enthusiasm.

She and Nadine settled on the couch and each bit into a fortune puff. "Um, yum," Nadine said. "Cream puffs are so much better without the black goo in them. That Homer's a genius."

At the mention of Homer, Katherine almost dropped her cream puff in her lap. "Homer made these?" she asked.

"Uh-huh," Nadine said. "This morning in Gladys's apartment."

"This morning?" Katherine leapt off the couch. "Is he still up there?"

"Oh, no, honey," Nadine said. "He's gone."

There was that word again. *Gone.* Katherine sank back onto the couch.

Nadine looked curiously at her. "What's up with you two? Every time I mentioned your name today, Homer just seemed to sag a little, poor guy."

Katherine nodded in understanding. She was feeling droopy herself. "I told him I wouldn't marry him."

"Oh, honey," Nadine said. "I'm sorry."

"Me, too." Katherine bit into her cream puff and noticed a piece of paper sticking out of the shell. "What's this?" she asked.

"The fortune," Nadine said. "Isn't that clever? Like I was about to say, that genius Homer decided we should put them in the shells, not the cream."

It certainly solved the ink problem. Katherine took out her fortune and read it aloud. "'The Ludlum reversible latch will be the toast of New York.' What does that mean?"

"That's where Homer went. He had an appointment this afternoon to sell his latch to a toy company in New York."

"New York?" Katherine popped up again, beside herself. "New York City?"

"Uh-huh," Nadine said.

"New York!" Katherine rushed to the closet and pulled out her suitcase.

Nadine got up and followed Katherine as she scurried around the apartment. "But honey, I don't think he's gonna be there too long. He said he was going back to Ludlum after that."

"It doesn't matter." Katherine couldn't believe those three words had come out of her mouth. So she repeated them. "It doesn't matter."

"Why doesn't it matter?" Nadine asked.

"Because I'll be in New York before he leaves."

The words shocked Nadine. "You're going to New York? Now? That doesn't sound like you!"

"Why not?" Katherine asked innocently. "I'm an old pro at road trips." She threw a sweater into her suitcase.

Nadine laughed joyously and gave Katherine a monster hug. "I knew it! I knew the minute I set eyes on you two that you were made for each other."

"Made to pester each other," Katherine corrected.

"That was just the trouble with Ned and me. We never really cared enough about each other to disagree on anything." Nadine looked at her watch. "You're going to have to hurry, though, if you're going to catch a train."

Katherine shook her head. "I don't think I could sit on a train right now. I know a better way."

"You're gonna fly?"

"I'm gonna drive."

Ten minutes later Nadine was on the sidewalk giving Katherine directions for pulling Bo Welton's rig into the heavy evening traffic. They'd been laughing nonstop, and Katherine still giggled even as she concentrated on getting the behemoth out of its tight parking space. Good grief. She'd lost her mind—and it was a great feeling.

Sitting on the Staten Island ferry at ten-thirty at night, Homer couldn't see any reason not to go back to Ludlum—except that Texas was an eternity away from Washington, and Katherine. But Katherine didn't want him. He had thought his trip to New York would make the parting easier. It hadn't. Twenty-four hours had passed since the last time he'd seen her, and he was still a wreck.

From a distance, Manhattan was beautiful. It was up close, too, if you considered a hubbub of humanity beautiful. Normally Homer did, but today his heart hadn't been in it. On his way to Whoopee-do Toys headquarters on Fifty-seventh Street, he'd hardly stopped to talk to a single person. He'd wrapped up his business quickly, making more money in that one afternoon than Grandpa Otis had ever dreamed of. But he didn't feel much like celebrating, and there was only one person he wanted to talk to.

One person—that was a new sensation. So badly did he want Katherine he could imagine giving up travel, his interviews for the paper, even his book, if only he could make a life with one stubborn woman in his sleepy little town. If he could just have Katherine, he wouldn't budge for the rest of his life.

But could he convince her of that?

Since he was a rich man now, Homer treated himself to a cab ride back to the Y. He watched the city pass by at breakneck, New York-cab speed, all the while wondering how long it would take to get to LaGuardia and from there to Washington. But then, what if he got to Katherine's apartment only to find that she hadn't missed him at all, or worse, that she'd been relieved he was gone?

"Will you look at this guy?" his driver bellowed, gesticulating so wildly they almost bumped into a city bus. "What kind of jerk parks an eighteen-wheeler in front of the Y? Those blasted trucks think they own the whole island!"

Clutching tightly to the door's armrest, Homer managed a sympathetic nod. It wouldn't do to tell the high-strung cabbie to slow down, he decided. The man might go ballistic.

"Why's a guy like that gotta stay at the Y in the first place? They got rest areas for those guys!"

As the cab braked to a stop near the Y, Homer reached into his pocket for the fare, glad to part company with the cranky driver. Then he spotted the truck the man had been griping about.

He threw way too much money in the plastic fare slot, leapt out of the car and inspected the huge vehicle. There was no mistaking it. The rig was Bo Welton's, and the only person who could have driven it to New York was Katherine.

"Homer!"

Katherine bounded off the stoop of the Y and ran to him, stopping just short of throwing herself at him. He took care of that, taking her light frame into his arms and swinging her in a full circle. He didn't know what she was doing here and he didn't care. He had to hold her.

Katherine's feet felt as though they might never touch ground again. "I was so scared I had missed you!"

"Katherine." Homer gestured toward the truck. "What have you done?"

She flashed him a smile and took his arm. "I went for a drive."

"You could have just taken a plane," he said.

"That wouldn't have been very adventurous."

Homer was speechless. He knew what he wanted to convey, but how?

Then he remembered what he had wanted to do last night outside her building before he had botched everything. In an instant he dropped down on one knee, grabbed Katherine's calves so she couldn't escape and looked up into her shocked eyes.

"Will you marry me, Katherine?"

Katherine clutched Homer's shoulders for balance. His words as much as his hands on her legs made her feel as if she'd lost her equilibrium. Her heart slammed against her ribs. This was what she wanted, had come here hoping for. But she'd also wanted to explain and apologize, assure him she could make it work between them.

Seeing the hesitation in Katherine's eyes, Homer blurted in a panic, "I'll stay in Ludlum with you forever, Katherine, I swear. I don't care if I never meet another person in my entire life or go anywhere. We don't even have to take a honeymoon."

"Homer..." Katherine looked at him warily, as if she was working up the nerve to say something. He hoped she wasn't working up the nerve to reject him. "Get up, Homer," she said.

Homer stood slowly. This was it, then. He'd just made a class-A fool of himself again for nothing. No, not for nothing—he'd had to try at least.

"Yes," she said.

He gasped. "You mean you're saying yes?"

"Yes. But now we've got a big problem."

Uh-oh. She'd marry him, but...what? He inhaled sharply. "What's the problem?"

"All the way down the New Jersey turnpike I was trying to plan our honeymoon. I've got some money saved, and I thought we could use it to take the mother of all road trips so you could get started on that book. I was even hoping to be your photographer.... But now I can see we're coming into this relationship with conflicting expectations."

Homer let out the breath he'd been holding and hugged Katherine with all his might. "I'm sure we can work something out," he said huskily. He was afraid he might crush her with all the joy welling up inside him.

"Let's get a cab."

Katherine stepped into the street and hailed a taxi—the same one that had driven Homer here.

"That was some reunion you two had. Made my whole day," the cranky cabbie said. "Where to?"

"Anywhere," Katherine said cheerily.

"Huh?"

Homer leaned forward. "Do you know where we could buy an engagement ring at this hour?"

"Well, congratulations!" The driver turned around and beamed briefly at them through the plastic barrier. "But if you wanna buy a ring, forget it. Where to?"

"Downtown," Katherine said.

"Uptown," Homer said at the same time.

The cabbie shook his head slowly. "Some marriage youse guys'll have," he said. "I'll take you to Greenwich Village."

Homer scooted closer to Katherine and took her hand. "I'll buy you a ring tomorrow."

"I don't need a ring, Homer," she protested.

"Oh, I forgot to tell you—we're rich."

"Rich?"

"Well," Homer amended, "by Ludlum standards, anyway." He told her the reason behind his journey to New York and about his sale.

"I'm happy for you," Katherine said. "And I'm glad you didn't give your latch to a company that wanted to make plastic guns for kids, even if it was my company. What did Whoopee-do want it for?"

"Some kind of new lifelike frog or some such. They say kids love 'em."

The cabbie slammed on the brakes, sending them both tumbling forward. "Washington Square," he announced. "Good luck."

Homer glanced at the fare meter and pulled out the right amount of cash. They took a leisurely walk through

Washington Square, stopping often to kiss and comment on the odd assortment of people still on the streets even though it was nearly midnight.

As they turned onto Sixth Avenue, Katherine was amazed by the number of people hocking their wares along the sidewalk, everything from yo-yos that glowed as they spun to old *Life* magazines. The smell of incense was pervasive and pungent in the night air. "This really is the city that never sleeps," she commented.

"It's a strange place altogether," Homer said.

"You must be tired of cities," Katherine said. "I bet you'll be glad to get back to Ludlum."

Homer hesitated. "That's true, but Katherine...well, I know you love Washington and your job—"

Katherine cut him off with a sharp laugh. "I think Bill Warren will be able to survive without me. He's company enough man for the both of us."

Homer was about to express his agreement when he realized he'd lost Katherine. He whirled around and saw her standing about ten feet back. She was staring at the pavement with tears in her eyes. He rushed to her side.

"Katherine, what's wrong?"

She shook her head in disbelief. Homer looked to where she was staring—an eclectic collection of books laid out for sale on the sidewalk.

"What's wrong?" he asked again.

"I can't believe it," she murmured. She picked up a book and held it reverently, her fingertip outlining its warped and water-stained cover, with its picture of a woman and several girls reading by candlelight.

"Is it a French book?" Homer asked.

"It has to be the one," Katherine said. She nervously thumbed to the flyleaf. Over her shoulder, Homer read the brief inscription written there: "To Katherine, Happy Birthday!"

"It was yours?"

"It's the copy of *Little Women* my mother gave to a Goodwill store in Ohio! That's my father's handwriting."

"It's still five dollars, lady," a man sitting nearby in a folded chair said.

"How did it get here?" Homer wondered aloud, rifling through his wallet for a five.

"I don't know." Katherine looked at Homer in disbelief. "I guess a better question would be, how did *I* get here?"

They both knew the answer to that, and memories of the past week made them laugh all the way up the street. They decided they should be married in Washington, with Nadine and Gladys in attendance, and then proceed to Texas.

"And then we can take that trip and start on 'The Plight of the Common Man,'" Katherine said.

Homer tugged her to a stop and kissed her forehead. "The book has to go on hold until we finish the house."

"What house?"

"Ours. The one we're going to build." He wrapped his arms around her.

"Oh, no," Katherine protested. "Don't tell me you're one of those people who believes in building their own house!"

"From the foundation up," Homer said. "It'll be a snap. And we can try these new solar panels I've been playing with."

Katherine groaned. "I hope it's going to be small."

"It's got to be two stories at least," Homer said, "for all the kids."

Katherine raised a quizzical eyebrow as her heart hammered against her ribs. "That's something we've never discussed."

"Well," Homer drawled in his best cowpoke accent, "it's not so much in the discussin' as in the—"

"Okay!"

"And I imagine we can be pretty inventive in that department, too."

Katherine threw back her head and laughed comfortably in his arms. "I don't care if we live in a solar-powered igloo and have dozens of unpatented kids. I love you, Homer."

After saying those four words, Katherine felt as if a hundred-pound weight had been lifted off her chest. She loved this man, and she was not only glad, but ecstatic that he wasn't a Hank or a Harold, or anything approaching the boring or practical.

"And I love you," Homer said. He tasted her lips briefly before they continued their journey up the avenue.

They walked almost the entire night, planning and talking and even arguing like an old married couple. They ducked down side streets and rested on park benches until dawn. When they saw the sun come up over the Fifty-ninth Street bridge, they headed back to the Y and pulled the parking tickets off the eighteen-wheeler.

"You want to drive?" Homer asked.

"Of course," Katherine answered brightly. "I'm an expert now."

She deftly pulled the monstrous vehicle away from the curb and settled in for a long drive. Neither of them was tired—they were both still too enthralled in the adventure they were embarking on. But then, Katherine suspected that the rest of their lives would be an adventure.

\* \* \* \* \*

## HE'S MORE THAN A MAN, HE'S ONE OF OUR

## MAD ABOUT MAGGIE
### by Pepper Adams

All at once, Dan Lucas was a father—and a grandfather! But opening his arms to his grandson didn't guarantee that he'd find a place in his son's life. And the child's aunt, Maggie Mayhew, would do anything in her power to keep Dan out of her family. But could she keep Dan out of her heart?

Available in October from Silhouette Romance.

Fall in love with our **Fabulous Fathers!**

FF1093

# Silhouette
# ROMANCE™

**THIS SIDE OF HEAVEN**

The miracle of love is waiting to be discovered in Duncan, Oklahoma! Arlene James takes you there in her trilogy, THIS SIDE OF HEAVEN. Look for Book Two in October!

## AN OLD-FASHIONED LOVE

Traci Temple was settling in just fine to small-town life—until she got involved with Wyatt Gilley and his two rascal sons. Though Wyatt's love was tempting, it was dangerous. Traci wasn't willing to play house without wedding vows. But how could she hope to spend her life with a man who swore never to marry again?

Available in October, only from Silhouette Romance!

## Silhouette Books has done it again!

Opening night in October has never been as exciting! Come watch as the curtain rises and romance flourishes when the stars of tomorrow make their debuts today!

*Revel* in Jodi O'Donnell's STILL SWEET ON HIM—
Silhouette Romance #969
...as Callie Farrell's renovation of the family homestead leads her straight into the arms of teenage crush Drew Barnett!

*Tingle* with Carol Devine's BEAUTY AND THE BEASTMASTER—
Silhouette Desire #816
...as legal eagle Amanda Tarkington is carried off by wrestler Bram Masterson!

*Thrill* to Elyn Day's A BED OF ROSES—
Silhouette Special Edition #846
...as Dana Whitaker's body and soul are healed by sexy physical therapist Michael Gordon!

*Believe* when Kylie Brant's McLAIN'S LAW—
Silhouette Intimate Moments #528
...takes you into detective Connor McLain's life as he falls for psychic—and suspect—Michele Easton!

Catch the classics of tomorrow—*premiering* today—
only from ⧖ *Silhouette*

Silhouette Books
is proud to present
our best authors,
their best books...
and the best in
<u>your reading pleasure!</u>

Throughout 1993, look for exciting
books by these top names in
contemporary romance:

**DIANA PALMER—**
*Fire and Ice* in June

**ELIZABETH LOWELL—**
*Fever* in July

**CATHERINE COULTER—**
*Afterglow* in August

**LINDA HOWARD—**
*Come Lie With Me* in September

When it comes to passion,
we wrote the book.

BOBT2